My Notebook

on

Prayer & Intercession

Suzanne Robinson Pollard

Our faith cannot be in ritual, tradition, or religion. Our faith must be in God alone.

"…I tell you the truth, if you have faith as small as a mustard seed, you can say to this mountain, 'Move from here to there' and it will move. Nothing will be impossible for you."

(Matthew 17:20)

In Christianity, the name of God is not a
human invention, but has divine origin
and is based on divine revelation.

I dedicate my words, thoughts and deeds
to the One True Living God, Who is God
the Father, Son and the Holy Spirit

Contents

You are UNIQUE

God looks through the physical being and sees your heart, spirit and soul.

He loves you because you are you.

You are not a surprise to Him.

Nothing you do will ever surprise Him.

He does not want you to compare yourself with others and judge yourself the lesser of the comparison.

He loves everything about you.

He will love you forever – warts (faults) and all.

No-one else sounds like you, cares like you, loves like you or gives like you.

He values you. He thinks you are worthwhile – and He is never wrong

Prologue

While attending an evening prayer meeting, my eyes were drawn to a young girl sitting in the back of the church. She was quietly, busily colouring in a picture book while she waited for her mother to finish leading the prayer group. I looked at her bowed head and I felt the Lord remind me of a verse I hold dear to my heart.

> Fathers (Mothers) do not exasperate your children; instead, bring them up in the training and instruction of the Lord.
>
> (Ephesians 6:4)

Then I felt Him speak into my heart, challenging me to think on my own children, and ask me how I could be sure that they understood the words they heard their mother use. Yes they mimic the words they hear me use but, as to whether or not they actually understood how to use them to God's Glory, I could not have accurately answered His challenge.

I felt the Lord say that it was the same with this young girl and most children who live in Christian households. Children grow up mimicking their parents in the hope that their parents will be pleased with them.

Parents hear their children use the words they use, and so rarely think to sit with their children and discuss how powerful words can be when used in prayer.

My heart was saddened at this lack on my part in not teaching my own children, but then grew silent as I felt the Lord direct...

'Teach my children about the importance of prayer and intercession in their daily lives. Teach them why they pray, how to pray, when to pray and what they pray'.

The more I allowed God to speak into this need to teach on these things, the more certain I became that these insights were not only for our children but for everyone interested in prayer and intercession.

Teach them how to worship the Lord their God through prayer and intercession. I desire that all my people would know that Prayer and Intercession is not just a weapon, or a plea for help it is a powerful tool of Victory. I desire that their voices would once again join with their hearts and return to a heart of worship –A heart of praise – a heart of prayer. A heart to seek to put Me in every part of their daily life.

Prayer is the greatest weapon we have against the evil one

As a Christian we pray knowing we do so in the power and authority found in our salvation through Jesus Christ, and not by our own strength or power.

The evil one has only one weapon – he whispers lies and deceit into our ears and causes us to doubt the truth of God's promises and word in our lives.

The evil one whispers in the hope we will not remember that he lost any hold over our lives over two thousand years ago when Jesus went to the Cross for us.

God did not want us to ever forget the battle has been won so He had it written into the scriptures long before Jesus came to earth.

God wrote it so that we can declare it into and over our lives knowing the evil one will be forever reminded that he has no part in the lives of us or our families. And so we are able to say it is written

> "...no weapon forged against you will prevail, and
> you will refute every tongue that accuses you.
> This is the heritage of the servants of the Lord,
> and this is their vindication from me," declares
> the Lord."

(Isaiah 54:17)

We are only the clay pot

As human beings created by God, we cannot heal by our words or our deeds.. God made us to be empty vessels He could fill with His love, His Power, His Grace and His Mercy to His Glory. Only God can heal people

> God can do anything…far more than you
> could ever imagine or guess or request in your
> wildest dreams!

> (Ephesians 3:20)

It is only by God's Grace and God's great Mercy we are able to see through the lies and deceit of worldly strife and hate to the love and peace God has for us.

Why does He heal? Because He loves us and He wants us to be well.

Does He always heal people in the way we want? No.

Sometimes He heals their *hearts* and not their bodies. We don't know why this happens but we have to trust God and thank Him for His peace to fill our own hearts as He helps us and the people we pray for to accept His answers to our prayer requests.

When we pray in Jesus' name we pray with the authority He gave us.

Jesus replied, "…and on this rock I will build my church, and the gates of Hades will not overcome it. I will give you the keys of the kingdom of heaven; whatever you bind on earth will be bound in heaven, and whatever you loose on earth will be loosed in heaven."

(Matthew16:17)

God heals because He loves us. This is how much God loves us – even though He stayed in Heaven – He sent His Son to redeem us from sin and His Spirit to guide us through life.

If you love me, keep my commands. And I will ask the Father, and he will give you another advocate to help you and be with you forever--He is the Holy Spirit, who leads into all truth...

(John 14:15-17)

Pray with a humble heart knowing that in your own strength you are able to do nothing. Because your heart was responsive and you humbled yourself...I have heard you, declares the Lord.

(2 Chronicles 34:27)

How do we humble ourselves? We come to God and are honest about how we feel and what we think.

It is only when we let the Holy Spirit guide our words and check our heart attitude are we able to speak with the authority and power found in the name of Jesus'.

Why did He have to die?

> But he was pierced for our transgressions, he was crushed for our iniquities; the punishment that brought us peace was on him, and by his wounds we are healed.
>
> (Isaiah 53:5)

According to Old Testament law people could only be forgiven their sins if they took an animal or bird to the temple to be sacrificed. This sacrifice was a life for a life. The animals died to pay for the sin of man. However this payment only covered the sin up to the day of the sacrifice. So, day after day, man would have to kill an animal or bird in the hope that his sins would be eventually forgiven forever.

Today the blood of an animal is no longer acceptable as a way to purify man's sins. God will only accept the blood of Jesus Christ as payment for the sins of man. Jesus came and offered His life as the last blood sacrifice that would ever be needed by anyone who wanted to be forgiven their sins against God. The bonus is that when we accept Jesus died in our place then we get the free gift of the Holy Spirit, who dwells in our hearts and helps us live a life knowing we are forgiven all our past, present and future sin when we confess them to God. The Holy Spirit in us encourages us to ask God to help us to do better the next time we are tempted. By choosing to do better we are able to be God's hands and feet on earth we are able to be God's hands and feet on earth.

At the end of Jesus' physical earthly ministry, God knew the enemy would want to come to rob, steal and destroy the relationship he had with his people. God accepted the sacrifice of His Son's earthly life as a substitute for everyone who would call Him Saviour. When we are one with Jesus we are empowered to use the authority of the Creator to break the power of darkness that tries to destroy our lives.

> Therefore God exalted him to the highest place
> and gave him the name that is above every name,
> that at the name of Jesus every knee should bow,
> in heaven and on earth and under the earth, and
> every tongue acknowledges that Jesus Christ is
> Lord, to the glory of God the Father.
>
> (Philippians 29-11)

This is part of *'the Power of Jesus'* we hear about - the power of healing, the power of forgiveness, and the power of new hope; the power of victory over darkness. We must remember to take everything to Him and offer it up to be washed in the blood-shed by Jesus on the Cross —every day – don't hold on to a little lie; or the theft of an extra biscuit; or a fight with your mum or dad – run to Jesus and ask Him to be in the middle of the situation and to forgive you, help you to forgive others and help you do better. (*I urge you to encourage your friends and family to go to Him too*).

When you are going to pray for someone –ask God to help you pray what He wants for the person –not what you want or what the person wants but what *God* wants for them

Remember there is absolutely nothing you can do to help the person in your own strength – so have peace that God has heard your prayers and knows what is best for the other person and He will provide what is needed.

Prayer should always and only ever be about exhortation encouragement, restoration, healing and God's love – only God has the right to chastise or bring correction to a person.

As a person of prayer, if I feel there is an uneasiness in a person or something awkward in a situation, the very first thing I need to do is to ask God to protect the person and intervene in the situation in the Name of Jesus and to bring rightness into being. We need to be open in our hearts and minds to discern the guidance of the Holy Spirit. So that we are praying God's Will for the person and into the situation.

Did you know?

God the Father - God the Son - and God the Holy Spirit known as the Holy Trinity are One Being – One Spirit?

Confusing – it was to me.

Then one day I bought a 'Get Well' card that had a single flower stalk with three rose heads on it and the Lord said to me "*that's how I am.*

I am One being but there are times when people have a call for the comfort and the love offered by the part of me that is Jesus–saviour, healer, redeemer, teacher and friend

And there are times when people need guidance, comfort, communication and friendship offered by the part of me that is the person of the Holy Spirit who dwells within them –

And then there is the need for the Father, the Creator of all, your provision and your provider, protector and safe harbour in times of stormy weather with a great desire to be a friend

I am One and I am All Do not worry when you pray who you should pray to – just know that when you seek the guidance and comfort of One you get the full attention of all."

What is Intercession?

*I*ntercession simply means you are praying for someone.

When *God* he sees someone is having a bad day and they need some help

He tells the *Holy Spirit*

Who in turn speaks it into *our hearts?*

If we our hearts are open to hearing, seeing the other person's need

And want God to help, heal or guide the other person

And we pray what is on our heart and thank God that He is already helping the person in need.

Jesus then takes it back to *God*'s heart from where the desire for prayer first started

This is called intercession - praying for someone else's need.

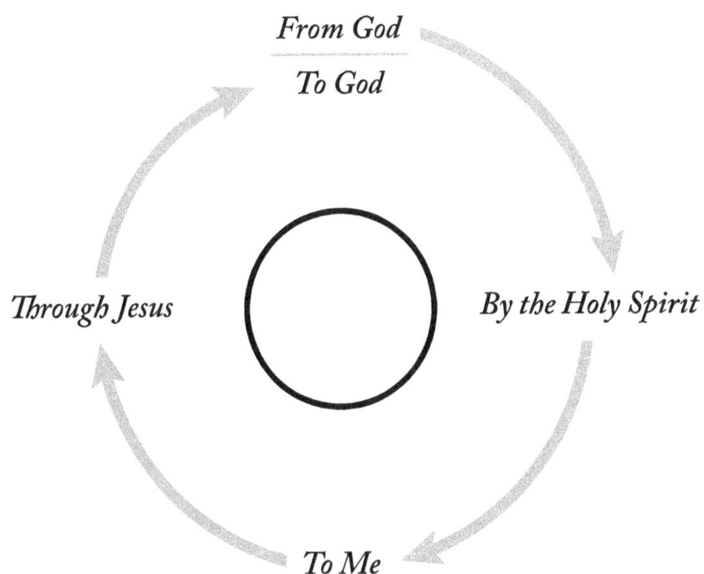

Prayer Wheel of Intercession
(Discovering the Secret to a Successful Prayer Life by Suzette Hattingh)

Who is called to be an Intercessor?

I am - You are - We all are

Why are we all intercessors?

Because every time we pray for someone we are interceding for them

We are going before *God* and asking, thanking Him for what he is doing in the person's life.

That is intercession.

How do we *intercede*?

We pray giving all the glory to *God* who is able to do all things and loves us so much that He invites us to be part of the miracle of answered prayer.

Why intercede for someone?

Simply because God wants us to:

◆ pray that everyone on the whole earth has the opportunity to know and love Him. Jesus directed to all who love Him

He said to them, "Go into all the world and
preach the gospel to all creation.

(Mark 16:15)

◆ help one and another by standing beside them and
asking God to help them when they are burdened
with the things of this world

Carry each other's burdens, and in this way you
will fulfil the law of Christ.

(Galatians 6:2)

When we said 'yes' to Jesus we asked Him to make
His home in our hearts, we became a house for Him to
dwell in.

And as he taught them, he said, "Is it not
written: 'My house will be called a house of
prayer for all nations'

(Mark 11:17)

How did we become intercessors?

Christ Jesus, who died--more than that, who was raised to life--is at the right hand of God and is also interceding for us.

(Romans 8:34)

When we accept what Jesus did for us and offer up our hearts to God we have the opportunity to become people of prayer. The Bible says to take everything to God in prayer and to seek Him through prayer.

Do not be anxious about anything, but in everything, by prayer and petition, with thanksgiving, present your requests to God.

(Philippians 4:6)

Jesus first interceded for us. Before Jesus came we were separated from God by a valley of sin that we could not cross. Jesus came and he bridged the gap for us. He died on the cross so that our sins could be forgiven forever. His body was broken –and His blood was spilled – He took the punishment of our wrong doings upon Himself and asked God to forgive us for not loving Him as we should. Jesus interceded on our behalf.

How did He come to do this for us?

When Adam and Eve disobeyed God and ate from the Tree of Knowledge a gap was formed between God in Heaven and Adam on Earth. The gap separated man from God's presence. The gap could only be crossed by people who were free of sin. Man tried for years to find forgiveness through their own effort but it was no good because in some way every single person on earth sinned against God in some way. So God sent His one and only Son to pay the full price demanded to make people clean of sin. This bridge, this way across the gap of sin, separating Heaven and Earth, was available for every person who accepted the *free* gift of His Son's life.

Why? It was the only way God could shows us He loves us and wants us to know and love Him. He sent His Son, Jesus, who stretched out his arms and made a way for us to cross from sin into relationship with *God*.

This is what intercession is – It is the opportunity we have to stand before God, having accepted Jesus into our hearts, and ask God to help someone else. **Why?** Because Jesus did it for us – and He is in us – we are able to stand before God and ask for help for our family and friends.

Everyone who accepts Jesus and all He did on the cross becomes an intercessor for the people around them.

Every time you pray for someone you are an Intercessor.

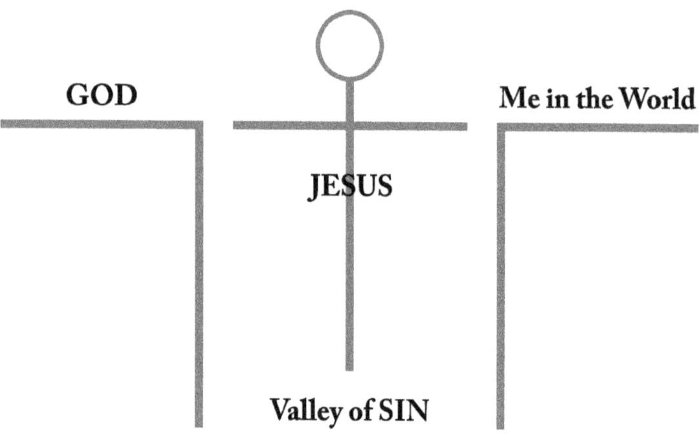

There is no way across *except* believing by faith that:

- Jesus paid the price to redeem me from a life of sin
- The price was His life
- He died for me so that I could come to know the loving acceptance of Father God for me
- He defeated death and rose again
- Jesus is alive and well and seated at the right hand of God in Heaven – there for me.
- He is the Son of God
- He is the Son of Man– He is one with us
- He is interceding for me –for you – for us.

"…we were by nature deserving of wrath. But because of His great love for us, God, who is rich in mercy made us alive with Christ even when we were dead in transgressions – it is by grace we have been saved. And God raised us up with Christ and seated us with him in the heavenly realms in Christ Jesus …

(Ephesians 2:3-6)

Faith – it is all about believing and accepting who Jesus is. For there is one God and one mediator between God and men, the man Christ Jesus

(1 Tim. 2:5)

When people say "go and tell the Good News to the world…"

Have you ever asked "what is the Good News?"

God cannot abide sin

You might ask "how can that be good news?"

Well it is not - the Good News is that Jesus came, lived on earth, and experienced life in a similar way as we are today. He came to tell us about His Father's love for us. And then He accepted God's plan for Him to die as payment for our sins.

You might wonder "why would God plan that?"

God wanted the people to love Him but he wanted them to choose to love Him, choose to know Him, choose to spend time with Him. We are the same we want the people around us to choose to love us, choose to be our friends.

When Adam and Eve, God's first friends, disobeyed Him and chose to eat the apple they discovered they were not the same as God, even though they wanted to be. They knew there were not good enough to be in His Presence (Genesis 3)

People tried for centuries to be good enough to be God's friend again and share His time and thoughts. Sometimes the people listened; and where able to live in peace and harmony, sharing their land and wealth. But it was no good because human nature is to look after ourselves before others. Time and time again all too soon men, and women, become jealous and greedy for what another person had and wanted it for themselves. (Kings I and II)

God knew the only way for people to find a way to live in peace was if He Himself paid the price of sin.

God could not come to earth because He is Spirit and too power full for humans to see Him. So He sent His Son tell us of God's love, grace and mercy, and gave us a way to be forgiven of our sins.

Jesus knew 'The Plan' included dying a horrible death, but he came anyway.

He *offered* His life so that we, you and me, would forever have a way to ask *and* receive forgiveness and be saved from an eternity away from God.

Because Jesus is part of God He did not die but showed us how death was defeated through Him; and how our spirits live on in Heaven. When we are given a gift by our family or a friend, it is because we are loved. We don't pay the giver for the gift but we accept it and offer our love and friendship in return.

The gift of salvation is free. We *cannot* earn it, nor do we have to pay money for it. It is a free gift because our Living God is full of Grace, Loving, Forgiving, Faithful and Merciful. We could never earn this gift of forgiveness, this gift of freedom to come to the Father whenever we want to.

What is prayer and why do we pray?

Prayer is lifting a person or a person's need up to *God*.

- Prayer is taking a need or a problem to *God* and asking for *His help*
- Prayer is standing in heart and in spirit with someone and asking God to meet their needs – whatever they are.
- Prayer is talking to *God* about our needs – trusting Him that He will answer our prayers, meet our needs in *His way*, in *His time* asking that *His will be done.*
- Jesus had a need in the Garden – a need not to go through the cross because he knew it would not be a good experience – but even then he prayed that not His will *but God's will be done.*
- We can ask, we can plead, we can petition God to do something – but our hearts must always be tuned into *God's* heart so that what we are actually praying is for *God's will* in the situation to be done.
- Remember that *God* does not always answer our prayers the way that *we think* He *should* – But He will always answer them in a way that is best for us and for *Him.*

Answered prayer *should always give the glory to God*

How do we know there is a need for prayer?

A person with a prayer need may come up to you and say

"I am having a problem and would like you to pray with me"

Or
"I have a friend who is having a problem and I would like you to pray with me for them"

Or
"My family is not happy so I would like you to pray with me for us"

They may or may not tell you what the problem is. *And* – this is a biggie –

You actually don't need to know what the problem is to be able pray for person up to *God* in prayer – it can help to know if there is specific need

But in reality you *don't* need to know – because God already knows of the need and the pain in the person, He is simply asking if you will bring it to Him.

God being *God* - doesn't really need our help to move in the situation *but*

And again here is the big thing: God wants us to share the joy of seeing answered prayer.

God invites us to be involved

God loves us so much, *and he trusts us* so much that He invites us to be *His* friend *and* stand with *Him* so that prayers can be answered.

How wonderful is that?

God trusts us with the hurts and needs of other people. He trusts us to stand with them and lift our hearts to God and ask Him to help them.

Prayer requests– prayer needs – and what we do with them is one way that *God* is able to check our hearts and our attitudes towards his people.

When someone is ill –

Do we thank God for healing them, asking him to meet their needs?

Or do we simply say *"oh isn't it terrible that person is ill"?*

When there is something bad happening in the world, or in our town or even in our own home – a fight, a sickness, a bomb, a terrorist attack, or a tidal wave – whatever it is

Do we simply say "oh that is terrible, it seems to be happening all the time, I wish it would stop?"

Or do we go to *God* and *thank Him* for stepping into that situation – thank Him that He is in the very middle of the situation and *His* hand is reaching out to everyone there and helping them.

Thank Him for bringing peace to a troubled family, healing to a hurting person, and practical help into areas of disasters.

God's Word tells us that God will bring good out of what the enemy meant for evil – when we believe in Him, trust Him and talk to Him about the problems we have in our lives.

> You intended to harm me, but God intended it
> for good to accomplish what is now being done,
> the saving of many lives.

(Genesis 50:20)

I believe with all my heart *this is what God wants* – He wants us, in faith and trust, to run to him with all problems and ask Him to help

These prayer needs can sometimes seem odd to us because God will often ask that we lift up to Him someone who is in trouble with the law.

Why?

Because *God* checks our heart attitude in relation to the person who caused the terrible thing as well as the people who have been hurt.

Why?

Because *God* loves all people – but he hates the sins that they do. *God* wants *all* people to come to accept His love to know His Son Jesus and what He did for them.

God asks us to lift up a person who has done bad things because He wants us *to have an open heart and an attitude where we are able to hear what it on God's Heart* and not just what is on ours.

This is prayer – being able to thank *God* that He is moving in all situations according to His goodness, *for His glory* so that *His will is done.*

Prayer is lifting up a problem or situation and *thanking God for God's will* in the situation.

We might think that we know what is right and How a problem should be fixed -Or- How a person should be blessed.

But *God* has *His way* of doing things -So at *all* Times- in *prayer*

As we give the problem to *God* - We give *thanks to God for* –His *healing*, His *help*, His *will to be supreme* in any and all situations. - It is only when we seek *God's* Will to be done are we praying God's way.

Did you know

Reading the bible aloud is *praying* God's promises and protection over you, over your family.

Read the Word – *Make the word of God personal,* after all *it was written for us –for you and for me.*

> I (say your name) am the body of Christ and Satan has no power over me. I overcome evil with good.
>
> (Rom. 12:21)

> Greater is He that is in me (say your name), than he that is in the world.
>
> (1 John 4:4)

What can we do when we pray?

- Some people go down on their knees
- Some people sit
- Some people lie on the floor
- Some people stand
- Some people walk about
- Some people pray with their eyes open
- Some people close their eyes – to help them focus on hearing God
- Some people put their hands together
- Some people hold their arms up
- Some people make the sign of the cross to acknowledge Father, Son and Holy Spirit
- Some people are loud
- Some people speak softly
- Some people cry
- Some people sing
- Some people are silent and wait to hear what the Lord wants to say
- Some people talk in their native language
- Some people pray in tongues – this is a language gifted through the Holy Spirit to our spirit.

- Some people call being able to speak in tongues as being 'Baptised in the Holy Spirit'. Others say 'filled with the Holy Spirit'.
- The Bible tells us this is a gift breathed into the disciples while they waited in the upper room after Pentecost.

> When the day of Pentecost came, they were all together in one place. Suddenly a sound like the blowing of a violent wind came from heaven and filled the whole house where they were sitting. They saw what seemed to be tongues of fire that separated and came to rest on each of them. All of them were filled with the Holy Spirit and began to speak in other tongues as the Spirit enabled them.
>
> (Acts 2v1-4)

- This gift of speaking in tongues is a gift of a language that cannot be understood by the enemy.
- Prayer offered up in this way is a special time between the Lord and you.
- When you *don't* know what to pray in your own language and you pray in tongues, you are able to pray asking for God's Will to be done and not yours.
- Praying in tongues is praying spirit to Spirit - your spirit to God's Spirit.

> For anyone who speaks in a tongue does not speak to men but to God.
>
> (1 Corinthians 14 v 2)

Gift of tongues

The gift of tongues is the Holy Spirit giving you the supernatural ability to speak in a foreign tongue that you have no knowledge or ability to speak out on your own. Only the Holy Spirit's supernatural transmission of this language out of your spirit will give you the ability to be able to speak this language.

There are two types of tongues He can give you. One is a tongue of this earth where you can speak a language that is not normal to you.

The other type of tongue that He can give a heavenly language that is not of this earth. The Bible tells us that there are "tongues of angels."

> If I speak in the tongues of men or of angels, but do not have love, I am only a resounding gong or a clanging cymbal.
>
> (1 Corinthians 13:1)

But in either event, it will be a foreign language that you will not be able to speak out on your own efforts, and it will be your own personal, private, prayer language between you, the Holy Spirit and the Lord.

Why would God even want us to have this kind of a gift?

I believe the reason is in the verse where it says that sometimes we will not know how to pray as we ought to.

> And the Holy Spirit helps us in our weakness. For example, we do not know what God wants us to pray for. But the Holy Spirit prays for us with groanings that cannot be expressed in words.
>
> (Romans 8:26 NLT)

A point of interest

The gift of tongues is different for everyone. The language of tongues is unique for every person, just as every person is unique to God. Our language can grow and change as we grow to know and love the Lord more.

Remember There is no right way or wrong way to pray – there is just the way you are most comfortable when you are praying.

Be aware that sometimes it is not appropriate to be loud – you *don't* have to be the loudest person in the room or group – sometimes you can be the softest and the quietest person there.

When we pray and seek Gods heart in a situation it can be *very private* and not something that we want to share – and this is ok too.

We need to be able to have quiet times with God when we pray. For God asks us to

"Be still and know that I am God".

(Psalm 46:10)

Prayer, for me, is going to God with thanksgiving and praise in my heart – thanking *God* that He has already answered the prayer I am offering up to Him.

Thanking Him that He

- is already in the situation
- has already fixed the problem
- has already met the need even though I can't always see it.

God checks our heart attitude to see if we are really able to trust Him to answer our prayer His way knowing it will be the best answer for all of us;

Or

whether we want Him to answer it our way so that we can actually see that He answered the prayer.

Because the thing with prayer is that *God hears* and *answers all prayer*– just not always in the way *we think* He should.

Ask and it will be given to you; seek and you will find; knock and the door will be opened to you. For everyone who asks receives; he who seeks finds; and to him who knocks, the door will be opened.

(Matthew 7:7-8)

The Enemy comes to *rob steal and destroy our homes and our families.*

He does this by trying to bring unhappiness into our homes and our friendships.

He tries to make it hard to get along with people at school and work

He tries to upset our mums and dads

He tries to upset us

He tries to upset our brothers and sisters

He tries to cause us to be jealous and envy our friends.

Remember when things just don't feel right turn to the greatest weapon you have to bring back peace and happiness into your life.

Call on the name of your Friend and Saviour, Invite Jesus into your day.

How can we know we are praying God's Will

The only way we know for sure that we are praying for God's Will to be done is when we:

- stop wanting people to see that we had any part in the problem solving process. We are not the power to heal or provide we are the simply the tool God can use to reach the hearts of people who have asked Him for help.

- do as Jesus did. We should end our prayers by asking for God's Will to be done. When we do this we are trusting, that even if we were off target in our prayer point, God is big enough to do what is best for the person we were praying for.

- pray for God's Will to be done and surrender the need we have to fix the problem through our own efforts.

> Our Father...Your Will be done on earth as it is in Heaven...

> (Matthew 6:10)

- listen to God with an open heart He speaks to us and invites us to offer up prayers to Him about what is on His heart. God only ever wants us to ask for good things for the people in our prayers. He will never ask us to pray for someone to be hurt.

◆ pray for a person, we can think we know what is best for them so, we pray asking God to do what we think would be best for them.

How can I pray for God's will to be done?

I find an answer to this question when reading how Jesus prayed in the Garden of Gethsemane. He knew his future on earth was short; he knew the pain he would go through on the Cross but even though He prayed asking if there was another way, Jesus surrendered His will to God.

> He withdrew about a stone's throw beyond them, knelt down and prayed, "Father, if you are willing, take this cup from me; yet not my will, but yours be done."
>
> (Luke 22: 41-42)

And so we also can pray in this way … *'but not my will Lord God but Yours be done in Jesus Name'* … We ask in this way because Jesus tell us

> Whatever you ask in My name, that will I do, that the Father may be glorified in the Son
>
> (John 14:13).

How can we know what to pray?

There are many ways to find out about a need for prayer.

- Someone may tell you of a need
- You might read something in the newspaper
- You might see a need or situation on TV
- You might hear about something on the radio
- You might see something that looks wrong and think that God needs to be in the situation
- you might think about someone you haven't seen for a while
- If we are open to praying with *God* He will bring people and situations to our thoughts

Or

- we will feel that something is not right with a person we see or know

  A personal example of this is when I felt a need to pray for people in Russia – *I did not know who they were but I know that God put an urgent prayer request on my heart for people living in a very small town in Russia – because I did not know the need or the people I lifted them up to the Lord and prayed in tongues so that I was able to pray in line with God's desires because I was praying in the Spirit through the Spirit to the Lord*

Or

◆ When you sit and *be still* in your prayer time with God, He may speak directly into your heart – or show you a picture. Asking for you to stand and pray for whatever it is that *God* has shown you.

◆ The Church family may call you to pray in a corporate way (together) or ask you to pray for people you don't know but who have asked for prayer.

◆ Your family may ask you to pray about something.

◆ Your friends may not ask you to pray but you might see or hear something that leads you to want to lift their situation up to the Lord and thank Him for being in their lives.

◆ There are many ways to hear about a need or a situation that we can pray for.

◆ Sometimes there is just a feeling that something is not right – you can't put your finger on it or even say what is making you uneasy this is also a time to pray.

  ◆ At this time, if you are anointed with the gift of speaking in God's own language (speaking in tongues) I would guide you to pray in this way. This way the need on God's heart is guided by the Holy Spirit to your spirit and you are praying in unison for the situation.

  ◆ If you have not as yet received the gift of tongues then I would guide you to *pray the Lord's Prayer* into the situation. Jesus gave us this prayer so that we could honour God, confess to God our sinful nature, offer to clear our heart of hardness and invite God into the situation. How wonderful is that!

Nothing is too small for His attention.

Make the Word of God personally powerful for to you and all you are praying for.

Did you know you can pray scripture?

Pray the scriptures over yourself and your family. Ask God to show you a passage or a Psalm and read it. Think on the verses do not rush the reading of them. By reading the words aloud you are able to hear what you say and think about what you hear.

I have found it matters little whether I read a whole chapter or just one verse to God – He just loves to hear me reading His Word. The Bible is all about God's promises to provide for and protect his people. When I pray from His word He empowers every word I speak to bring healing and restoration to those I pray for.

He will do this for you too, if you are willing to try it.

In all your ways acknowledge him, and he will
make your paths straight

(Proverbs 3:6)

Do you go to God with everything you need help with?

Do you sometimes think… God is so busy looking after the whole world that your problem is too small and unimportant for you to bother Him about it?

Do you think you are wasting God's time when you ask Him to help you find a lost piece of paper, a lost family pet, a lost ring or necklace?

Do you spend so much of your time and energy trying to fix your own problems, your relationships that you simply forget to ask God to help?

God cares about you. God loves you.

God wants to share every moment of your life with you.

God wants to help you in every way – every day – with everything.

He just wants you to ask Him to help – He is just waiting for you to invite Him to help you live your life.

Why does He wait? - *Because He is a gentleman.* He will never bust down the door and intrude on your life. He wants to be *invited* into your Life. He wants to be invited to help your with your problems.

How can we pray?

*S*o what shall I do?

> I will pray with my spirit, but I will also pray with my mind; I will sing with my spirit, but I will also sing with my mind.

> (1 Corinthians 14:15)

- Prayer can be sung
- Prayer can be thought
- Prayer can be felt
- Prayer can be loud
- Prayer can be soft – soft as a whisper
- Prayer can be in your native language
- Prayer can be in *God's* language (Speaking in Tongues)
- Prayer can be sitting thinking on God
- Prayer can be a combination of all of these
- Prayer can be one of thankfulness - just for being,
- Prayer can be one of crying out to God when we are upset or hurt
- Prayer is putting us in a place where God can reach in and place *His* desire – *His* need for His people into our hearts.

Prayer is always a choice – we can choose to lift up a need on our heart to God or not. God hopes that we will choose to hear Him, hear the needs of our friends, family members, our town, our country, our world and bring them before Him

> Enter his gates with thanksgiving and his courts with praise; give thanks to him and praise his name.
>
> (Psalm 100:4)

> I will sacrifice a thank offering to you and call on the name of the Lord.
>
> (Psalm 116:17)

It isn't wrong to pray for ourselves.

God wants us to bring our needs and even our wants to Him. The Bible says,

> "Do not be anxious about anything, but in everything, by prayer and petition, with thanksgiving, present your requests to God"

(Philippians 4:6).

God knows our needs and sees our wants. He meets our needs but sometimes, for our own good, God holds back on giving us all our 'wants'. When we pray, we need to know that *His answer* to our prayer might be No, or Not Yet. *When we pray we have to trust God to know what is good for us.*

When can we pray?

All the time – Is the answer I would give. Prayer in our lives should be as normal as breathing.

Just as you are able to walk and talk; ride a bicycle and see all that is around you; watch television and talk with your family; organize food for the family dinner and cook more than one thing at a time; so too you are able to go about your daily life and still be able to lift up prayer for the people you see around you.

Prayer can begin when you wake in the morning and continue throughout your day until you close your eyes at night.

- We pray as we start the day and invite the Lord into our day – asking Him to prepare our way and to be in the middle of every situation and circumstance.
- We pray over our food, thanking God for His bounty and asking Him to bless it to our bodies and bless the hands and provided it.
- We pray while we are driving
- We pray when we take exams
- We pray when we are at work or playing with our friends in a park.
- We pray when someone is hurt

- There are times when we gather together for a prayer night at church or meet in small groups to pray.
- We can pray when we on top of a mountain or walking for exercise or shopping.

God is calling each and every one of us to pray *all* the time, because when we pray we are talking to Him.

I believe that the Lord is asking that we live with prayer in our hearts so that when there is a need – when there is a problem – when someone is hurt we are already in a position to simply lift up the need to the Lord and He is just there with us, waiting to talk to us.

God sent His Son Jesus so that we would know He wanted us to have a relationship with Him. For me that relationship is a personal place where I am aware of God is my best friend, where I am able to share what I think with him and He is able to share what is on His heart with me.

By spending time with Him we grow to know his touch in our hearts and recognise His voice when He calls. *"My sheep hear My voice, and I know them, and they follow Me..."* (John 10:27). When we pray we should be able to slip into our personal place with God without feeling like we need to prepare ourselves with ritual preparations and petitions for God's attention. *Just ask Him*

So when can we pray?

- When we are crossing a road - Or waiting at traffic lights - Or walking down a street – when we see and ambulance or a fire truck.
- That is a time for prayer. Pray that the Lord protect all who use the roadways both here and throughout the town. Thank Him for protecting the roads; thank Him that He will reach in touch the hearts of all who travel on them so that they will be open to His Word in their lives.
- When we are shopping, or at work or at school or at play – call on the Lord to touch all who also go to these places, ask for his blessing over everyone, ask for His healing touch in their lives and ask that he would open their eyes and their hearts so that they may come to accept Jesus and know His love.

You see there is not a time when we should *not be praying*. For all around us there is a need for prayer and all around us God is putting the needs of the people on our hearts – when we are open to *Him* – when we are listening to Him and sharing our lives with Him then we too become aware of the needs of the people around us.

All the time is a good time for prayer.

Today Christians worldwide pray to God by uttering the familiar words,

"Our Father in heaven, hallowed be your name, your kingdom come, your will be done, on earth as it is in heaven.

Give us today our daily bread. And forgive us our debts, as we also have forgiven our debtors.

And lead us not into temptation, but deliver us from the evil one."

(Matthew 6:9-13)

We know this prayer as the Lord's Prayer.

In it we call out to God and acknowledge who *God* is – He is our Father in Heaven - and just as we call out to our friends to get their attention so too does *God* know we are talking to *Him* when we call out to Him by name saying…"*Our Father, who is in heaven*"

But just calling to Him isn't enough we need to praise Him by acknowledging how much we honour his name so we say…"*Hallowed be thy name*"

We tell God what we want most and that is to live with Him as King of our heart and our lives. He rules a Heavenly Kingdom which is all around us. When we make Him our

King then we are asking that He dwell with us and that we dwell with Him so we say let …"*Thy kingdom come*"

We tell Him of our desire for His Will to be in every situation and circumstance of our lives by inviting …"*Your will be done in Heaven and on Earth*"

(Where is Earth? Earth is around us but also in us – we were made of the earth- read Genesis where God created Adam – the cry of our hearts can be for God's Will to be done in 'us' as well as all around us.)

We ask that God keep us on track – keep us close to *Him* - by feeding us His word daily we say…"*Give us our daily Bread*"

(Our body needs food daily so does our spirit need feeding daily. It is our choice to nourish our spirit and soul no one makes us read the Bible - but reading the bible daily encourages us and gives God a way to talk to us through His word)

We know that the only way God can answer our prayer is if we are willing to be like Him – what did he do that we can do? He forgave us – He wants us to do the same? So with a willing heart we call out …"*Forgive us our sin*". and as a sign of our willingness to be like God we add… "*even as we forgive others*"

(Often people question 'How many times must I forgive someone?' Jesus told us seventy times seven –every single

thing every single day. I believe He knew that one of the worst things that could happen was for a heart to become hard, bitter and resentful – in this prayer Jesus encourages us to always walk forgiving other people who hurt and disappoint us, and to forgive ourselves when we realise that we have done something wrong. If God's grace and mercy can offer us forgiveness then His hope is that we should want to forgive too.)

We are able to seek God's protection, discernment and help in not doing wrong things by asking Him to…*"Keep us from all evil and deliver us from sin"*

And we then acknowledge that *God* is able to do all things for all time we honour Him by praying … *"For thine is the power and the glory forever and ever."* And every one who agrees says- *"Amen"*.

Do you know the role of a Father?

A Father's role is to feed his household: physically and spiritually. He loves and cares for this household because it is His.

God as your Heavenly Father loves you unconditionally and *there is nothing you can do to make God love you more than He does right now*– equally there is *nothing you can do that will ever make Him love you less.*

There is nothing He does not know about you.

You are not a surprise to Him equally - *Nothing you do is a surprise to Him.*

He is your Heavenly Father; He knew you before you were born; He knows who you are and He loves you.

How can we know God as our father?

We must first know His Son, Jesus Christ.

> Jesus said '...you know the way to the place where I am going' Thomas said to Him '...how can we know the way?" Jesus answered, "I am the way and the truth and the life. No one comes to the Father except through me.

> (John 14:2-6)

Where can we pray?

Most times we will find ourselves praying in our homes, our churches, meeting in places to pray for an area or a place.

Wil Pounds in 2006 wrote in *Reflections for the thinking person*.

The place where we pray is insignificant as long as our prayers are offered to God the Father on the basis of the death of Jesus Christ.

When our life is one of prayer, meaning we walk with a heart to serve the Lord then we are ready to pray wherever we are. And we can pray for people wherever they are, we *don't* have to be in the same room for God to move and touch their lives. (http://www. abideinchrist.com/selah/sep28.html)

Prayer is the thought, the word, which carries a concern, a need or a thank-you to God.

It can be watching someone driving recklessly and we think "Oh Lord help that person arrive safely and help all the other people on the road with them"

It can be waiting at a traffic light to change and you see a mum having trouble with her children and we think "Oh Lord please help the children behave" or

"Please Lord give the person wisdom in how to parent her children."

It could be seeing a friend struggling with homework or an exam, or a work situation and we think "Help them Lord, to have peace and knowledge to deal with their problem."

These are not selfish prayers but prayers asking for the Lord to intercede in the situation and circumstances of some-one else.

We might see something on television and ask the Lord to be in the middle of the situation so that He can bring about a good solution to glorify His name.

God is the God of all possibilities

God is the God of impossible situations

God is every-where all the time – because He is spirit and does not have to be physically in a place to be able to answer prayer for that place or person. (I know that is a big thing to think about but God is not like us – He was not born to live on Earth – He already existed and He exists today – just as He did yesterday and just as He will tomorrow.

And the best thing is *God* is waiting to hear us ask, thank, and praise Him for every need, everything around us.

So where can we pray? *Anytime ... Anywhere*

Why do we pray together

God hears all prayer - this is true. He hears us when we pray on our own.

And He hears us when we join with our friends and family to pray in groups.

Jesus actively encouraged his disciples to pray together by telling them

> "Again, I tell you that if two of you on earth agree about anything you ask for, it will be done for you by my Father in heaven.
>
> ...For where two or three come together in my name, there am I with them."
>
> (Matthew 18:19-20)

There is *power in agreement.*

> "How should one chase a thousand, and two put ten thousand to flight...." One can put a thousand to flight, and two can put ten thousand to flight.
>
> (Deuteronomy 32:30)

...for where two or three come together...
(Matthew 18:19-20)

The most powerful union in prayer is when I stand with the Father, Son and Holy Ghost and pray what is on His heart.

Sometimes when I go out the front of the church for prayer, no-one one comes to pray with me. The first time this happened I was upset and on the point of feeling rejected and hurt when the Lord spoke into my heart and said...

> *...Suzanne it is I who have kept them away from you at this time for I am a jealous God and I wanted My words to be the only words you heard into your heart and your situation at this time.*
>
> *Do not hold hurt for being over-looked rather pray thanking the people for listening and being obedient to the voice of God by leaving you alone at this time.*

There is no one I would rather receive prayer from than the Lord Himself.

Prayer and Intercession in Holy Communion

Jesus took the bread; and when He had given thanks to God for His bounty, He broke it and said, "This is My body, which is given for you; *do this in remembrance of Me.*"

In the same way He took the cup also after supper, saying, "…This cup is the new covenant in My blood; do this, as *often as you drink it, in remembrance of Me.*" (1 Corinthians 11: 24)

1 Corinthian 11:27 talks of the judgement we bring upon ourselves when we come to the communion table with fault in our hearts.

Sharing Holy Communion with God is something I would never be able to do under my own efforts, for I would never be sin-free enough to be acceptable to Him. My thoughts and my feels, towards others and myself, are always sinful. My humanity causes me to be jealous, envious, judging and judgemental.

Yet today I am able to take communion without hesitation and with joy and thanksgiving at every opportunity.

You may ask *why* or *how can you do this?* The answer is simple I remember it is not for me to judge or be judged, by others or myself.

Jesus died for me when I was still in sin. He accepted me as I was, He accepted me when I offered to do better. *He offered to intercede for me* and help me stay on track with doing better in my life so; I ask *Jesus* to look into my heart and to challenge everything I hold inside of me.

I ask Him to forgive my misdeeds and help me forgive others who have hurt me; *then I think of Him and remember that he died for my sins,* He shed His blood for Me and I carefully regard His gift of salvation. *I pray thanking Him,* thanking God the Father- who was, is and is to come for the love they have for me.

I found no better way to grow in my relationship/ friendship with God than to set aside time to take Communion in my own home with Jesus.

I don't always have bread or wine at home so I take a biscuit and some water. Then I thank Jesus for the biscuit and the water and dedicate them to Him by asking they be acceptable to be used to renew my commitment to God the Father, Son and Holy Spirit. *Then in faith I continue.*

When I take communion at home it *is not about whether I use wine/water or bread/biscuit it is about remembering Jesus and what He did for me on the Cross at Calvary.*

Do not wait until you think you are ready to pray

I am not perfect and *surprise!* You will probably find that neither are you. We never will be.

Only Jesus is perfect, without sin. I know I sin in little ways all the time so I am always going to God and asking His forgiveness and help to do better.

If I waited until I was perfect enough (in my own mind) to pray what is on God's heart then I never would pray.

Interceding, praying is not about me being perfect; it is about offering up a willing heart to stand with God for the need that is on His heart.

Praying is about taking a step of faith knowing, trusting in your heart of hearts that the Lord God sees you and, because you accept who Jesus is and what He did for you, God accepts you as righteous and pure enough to come before him with your petitions of needs and wants.

Only the righteous and pure of heart are able to be in the presence of the Lord God Almighty.

Only one man has ever been wholly without sin and pure of heart.

And He paid *the price of our sin which is death.* He redeemed us from a life-time in hell. He offered

Himself to be the only sacrifice we would ever have to know, make or give. He sacrificed His life on Earth – *we are asked to sacrifice our self-will* by choosing to know, love and honour the One True Living God; holding nothing above Him in our hearts or our lives.

When we do this we are the righteousness of God through Jesus Christ and we go to God the Father, Creator of the Heavens and the Earth giving praise for His Son.

> To him who is able to keep you from stumbling and to present you before his glorious presence without fault and with great joy- to the only God our Saviour be glory, majesty, power and authority, through Jesus Christ our Lord, before all ages, now and forevermore! Amen.
>
> (Jude 1v24-25)

How Do We Prepare for Prayer

There are as many ways to prepare to pray as there are individual people on the earth.

My suggestions would be for you to find somewhere you are able to quieten your mind and focus on God. This place could be a room or under a tree or by the beach or in a café having a drink.

> "But when you pray, go into your room, close
> the door and pray to your Father, who is unseen.
> Then your Father, who sees what is done in
> secret, will reward you."
>
> (Matthew 6v6)

Praise Him. He is the Creator of all things great and small.

> "Enter his gates with thanksgiving and his courts
> with praise; give thanks to him and praise his name."
>
> (Psalm 100v4)

Sometimes you may not sing or say thanks – sometimes you can just offer God a heart full of love for Him. - Read the Word of God. - Think on what you read.

Know you have the same Spirit in you that raised Jesus from the dead – you carry the authority of a child of the Most High God and demons must flee when you stand with God and speak the Name of Jesus.

"Submit yourselves, then, to God. Resist the devil, and he will flee from you."

(James 4v7)

Ask God to write His Words on your heart so that you know who you are in Him and who He is in you. - Give God a chance to speak into your heart by setting aside some time to

"...be still and know that He is God".

(Psalm 46:10)

This time of stillness will depend on you and God – time is irrelevant to the Lord but He does know we have timetables so sometimes you may only be still for a few moments.

Put on some worship music and enter into His Gates with praise and thanksgiving

- When you live a life where thanking God for everything in your life is natural
- When you have asked God to touch your heart with His compassion and His love for people

- When you choose to hear the Holy Spirit speak into your heart
- When you immediately take what you hear to Jesus
- When you wake each morning knowing it's a glorious day just because by the Grace of God you woke up.

Then you are already prepared to pray - You are living a life of prayer. You *don't* have to find His presence, you are already in it.

A point to remember whether praying alone or in a group submit your heart to the Lord so that you are able to pray in accordance with His Heart and His Will for the situation.

How can we do this?

How can we know our hearts are submitted to God?

Before we pray we can ask God to search our hearts and show us if we are holding any anger, hurt, rejection, disappointment, jealousy, or un-forgiveness and ask Him to forgive us for holding on the pain and to heal us. *And* we ask Him to help us to forgive the people who have hurt and disappointed us.

Forgiving someone who has hurt you is hard.

If it was easy God would not put as much value on it as He does.

Why is it important to God?

God wants us live with peace and joy in our hearts. When we carry around hurt inside us it changes the way we see the world God made.

When we stop seeing His beauty all around us we stop wanting to talk to Him.

Why do we stop talking to Him? Because in some strange way we blame Him for the darkness and the pain we see all around us. And we forget that it is our own un-forgiveness that caused the darkness in the first place.

God wants us remember He forgave our sins two thousand years ago.

And He forgives us today, every time we deny Him we reject His Grace and Mercy working in our daily lives.

He forgives us when we talk badly about Him.

He forgives us when we blame Him for the bad things that happen in our lives and in the world.

Because God forgives us all these things He wants us to forgive the people who hurt us; He wants us to ask Him to help us forgive those who hurt us.

God knows this is hard to do but all He is asking is that we *try*. Just by saying '*Lord I want to forgive but the hurt is too much and I can't*' is the first step to forgiving. Asking Him for help takes us to a place where, over time, we can learn to forgive unforgiveable hurts. We do this with God's love and God's help.

How long should my prayer be?

Don't be fooled into thinking prayer must be long and lengthy and full of scriptural quotations and big words. There are times when God will fill your heart with His passion, compassion and longing for people to know Him and your prayer may be long and full of scripture; sometimes even full of tears for the lost.

There are times when you are called to warfare, fight for a situation in the spiritual realm, and are filled full of the power of the Holy Spirit as you rise up and stand in the path of the evil one and tell him as Jesus did.

> Jesus said to him, "Away from me, Satan! For it is written: 'Worship the Lord your God, and serve him only." Then the devil left him, and angels came and attended him.
>
> (Matthew 4v10-11)

When you are guided by the Holy Spirit in you, you will know what to pray. Prayer is not wrong when it comes from your love of God *and* when you pray for His Will to be done.

Prayer can be long, loud, short, or softly spoken. Prayer is as individual as the person praying.

Warning: The evil one will try to distract your prayer, and may even cause you to doubt what you are praying, because he does not want you to be confident in your prayer life. If He has you doubting your thoughts and words then he has won because when we are not confident that we hear from God we stop praying.

You *do not need to justify your words or argue* or with the devil. The evil one has no right to know why you chose those words, or why *you think* he desires to be banished from your presence.

So when you feel strife around you, say with authority "Satan, *In the name of Jesus be gone from this place.*"

There will be times when you will keep your prayer short and say '*Lord thank you for being in that person today, or thank you for meeting all their needs this day.*' You might see or think of something and simply breathe the name of '*Jesus*' -releasing His power to do what needs to be done.

Jesus gave us a way to pray in the Lord's Prayer. When you feel God's Heart for prayer I believe you will pray until He takes that prayer need away from you. Might be a few minutes, might be hours or days.

From early times priests and ministers have helped people to pray by teaching prayers for different occasions and celebrations. Today these prayers are still being prayed and still being heard by God.

How long do I pray for the same thing

> … DO NOT use vain repetition. DO NOT ask for earthly things; your Father knows what things you need to carry out the things he wants you to do.
>
> (Matthew 6:5-8)

Jesus talked about persevering when he told the parable of the widow who continuously put her petition to the judge until she got her answer.

Then Jesus told his disciples a parable to show them that they should always pray and not give up. He said

"In a certain town there was a judge…and there was a widow in that town who kept coming to him with the plea, 'Grant me justice against my adversary.'

"For some time he refused. But finally he said to himself…because this widow keeps bothering me, I will see that she gets justice,

so that she won't eventually wear me out
with her coming!"

(Luke 18:1-5)

All I can say is - *pray until God gives you peace* about the person or thing you are praying about. Then thank Him, for the answering your prayer.

Do you know God as your Heavenly Father?

For many years I believed God was in the sky and was watching over me from a distance. I would look into the sky when I was talking to Him, trusting He could see me, hoping He would hear me.

Then one day He touched my heart and let me see that He is here with me, in me and around me. He showed me He was someone I could go to when I was hurt or upset, and He would comfort me as a parent would. He became real to me.

Remember who you are when you pray.

Remember why you have the right and the power to tell the devil to leave you, and all you pray for alone.

You are the righteousness of God in Jesus Christ
(2 Corinthians 5:21)

You can do all things through Christ who strengthens you
(Philippians 4:13)

You are submitted to God, and the devil flees from you because you resist him in the Name of Jesus.
(James 4:7)

You have received the power of the Holy Spirit to lay hands on the sick and see them recover; to cast out demons and speak in tongues
(Mark 16:17)

You have the power over all the power of the enemy, and nothing shall by any means harm you.
(Luke 10:19)

You can quench all the fiery darts of the wicked one with your shield of faith
(Ephesians 6:16)

God is not deaf

God is not slow in knowing what it is you are praying. God does not need to be told over and over again. *He hears you the first time.* So unless He puts it upon your heart to repeat your prayer move on to the next thing you want to take to the Lord.

You do not need to copy people -Just because someone else prays in a way that you think sounds good does not mean that *you* have to pray the same way.

You are unique there is no-one else like you. In the whole world only one person can do what you can do and God wants to hear you pray, not hear you imitate someone else. Trying to sound like someone else is like trying to play hide-and-seek in a glass house with God.

God knows every voice on earth, past present and future to Him your voice when you pray; sing or just talk to Him makes the most beautiful sound His ears have ever heard. He loves the way you pray He hears you and He will answer all your prayers in a way that is best for the person and situation and to glorify His Holy Name.

What do we do after we have prayed?

We thank God for the work He has already done.

- We are able to do this when we remember Jesus *did it all* on the cross over 2000 years ago.
- He took all our sin – All our disease and illness - All the hurts of the world into Himself - allowed His body to be beaten and broken and nailed to a cross.
- He descended into hell - 'kicked' devil butt and took back the keys to God's Kingdom.

> "Therefore He says: When He ascended on high, He led captivity captive, and gave gifts to men. Now this, "He ascended" – what does it mean but that He also first descended into the lower parts of the earth?"
>
> (Ephesians 4:8)

- This is why we thank God for our answered prayer – because every battle we are in – every attack planned by the evil one – has already been won by Jesus.

We ask and thank God for His peace and His strength to fill us so that we are able to take our hands off the situation and *trust* Him to answer our need or our family and friends need.

I found this was hard to do – to let go of the problem and let God be God. But this is what we have to do. Pray, Give it to God, Let go and Trust Him.

How do we know we have let go of the problem?

When we give the problem to God, we should be able to stop worrying about it and thank Him that He is in control of the situation whenever we think about it.

How do we know we have released the prayer need to God? We should have peace in our hearts (*even though we may keep thinking*) about people and their circumstances. This is natural, because once we know something it is very hard to stop thinking about it; even harder still to not try to find a way to fix the problem involved. The evil one will even try to tell us that we have not done enough to help *but this is not true* – we have done the most important thing we can. *We prayed* and we gave the problem to God to answer.

You might ask - **How can know I have actually let go of the problem?** I found this was hard to do until I heard of something that allowed me to visualise the difference between trying to let go of something and actually letting go.

I was told to hold a pencil between my thumb and fore-finger and hand it to another person but when they took hold of the pencil I was not to let go of it. I realised that if I never actually took my fingers off the pencil then I never gave it away. *Until* I opened my fingers I was still holding the pencil.

Now, when I am not sure I have given the problem to God I pick up a pencil, reach out and place it on a table then I let go and say '*There you are Lord I have taken my hands off the problem so that you can go to work on it*'.

As soon as you have prayed what is on your heart *surrender* the prayer need, and the person, to God and leave them there with Him. Pray as God leads, Rest in His presence until He calls you to pray with Him again.

Caring about other people and their situations is good but we can become physically sick and spiritually tired if we try to carry another person's load. Jesus said… "Come to me, all you who are weary and burdened, and I will give you rest. Take my yoke upon you and learn from me, for I am gentle and humble in heart, and you will find rest for your souls. For my yoke is easy and my burden is light." (Matthew 11v28-30)

Today there are wars and natural disasters happening all over the world and it is very easy to take the killings and loss of homes to heart. *We can even begin to think that there is no good thing in this world* and become overwhelmed with all the bad stuff that is happening.

Unfortunately, when we try to fix the world's problems on our own prayers and strength we forget to see the good around us. We forget to see the sun is shining and that God is working even if we do not see it happening.

We forget to give the problem to God and let go.

We forget to *trust* God to bring us all through the dark times.

Do you have a problem you think is just too hard to deal with?

Try physically giving it to the Lord
- Make yourself a small box with a lid to fit then wrap it in party paper
- Get a pen or thick indelible pen
- Write on the box in *big bold* letters SFGTD
- This stands for something for God to do.
- Now write a note to God tell Him the problem – fold up the note – lift the lid of your SFGTD box and put the note inside then close the box.
- Don't check on the note *but* trust God to be working for you.
- Then allow peace in your heart knowing you have physically given God your need and left it in His hands to give you the help you need.

Keys to the Kingdom

What are the Keys? My understanding is they are the Power of God and the Authority of Man united in Jesus and given to those who accept the work of the Cross.

What do we use them for? We stand in the Authority and Power with Jesus to bring God's peace and love into places being attacked by darkness and pain.

Why did we lose this power? God gave mankind the authority over every living thing on earth How wonderful and powerful is that – the right to rule with God's compassion and love in their hearts.

> Then God said, "Let us make mankind in our image, in our likeness, so that they may rule over the fish in the sea and the birds in the sky, over the livestock and all the wild animals, and over all the creatures that move along the ground."
>
> (Genesis 1:26)

But so that man would know he was answerable to God, He gave them a condition to their freedom to rule…"the Lord God commanded the man,

> You are free to eat from any tree in the garden; but you must not eat from the tree of the knowledge of good and evil…"
>
> (Genesis 2:16-17)

When they disobeyed God they lost their place next to God and they lost the gift to Satan who used it to cause harm to man whenever he could.

How did we get them back?

God knew there was only one way for man to find his way back to a relationship with Him – He *had to* send His Son, Jesus.

Jesus became *Son of man*, died as *Son of man*, descended into Hell and took back the *Authority of Man* that Adam and Eve had lost through disobedience. Then He *rose as the Son of God*.

When I accepted Jesus as my Saviour, my authority is reinstated. When my heart is right and I seek God's Will, I am able to *stand with Jesus in the Authority of Man and the Power of the Holy Spirit to defeat the enemy.*

Jesus replied, '... And I tell you that you are Peter, and on this rock I will build my church, and the gates of Hades will not overcome it. I will give you the keys of the kingdom of heaven; whatever you bind on earth will be bound in heaven, and whatever you loose on earth will be loosed in heaven.'

(Matthew 16:18-19)

How can we be strengthened to pray?

I find I am both strengthened to pray and refreshed in body and spirit by spending time with God. Being quiet with God enables me to see His beauty and hear His voice. Hearing from God, receiving prayer from God can be as gentle as sitting in His presence.

How do we do this?

Mostly we decide to spend time talking to God and waiting on 'hearing' Him' talk back to us.

He loves it when we sit silently and wait on Him.

God may speak to you at this time through thoughts or pictures or feelings

God may simply whisper He loves you and make you feel nice inside and out (for me this is when He is holding me and just letting me rest with Him)

Other times He may put a prayer need on your Heart and you can lift up the need to Him.

Other ways we can be refreshed are when we
- put on some worship music
- read a passage in the Bible and think about what it means to us

- thank God for what He is saying to us through the verses we read.
- begin by thanking the Lord for all that He is and has done for us
- thank Him for his protection, provision in our lives, in the lives of our family and friends
- thank Him for our country – for the leaders of our country
- thank The Lord for a beautiful day – for a good day at school – for good friends
- thank Him for the things we want Him to be in – for example you could

  'Thank the Lord He is with you today'

  Thank the Lord for a good result in your test'

  Thank the Lord for healing your Grandma'

There are so many things we can thank Him for. God loves us to come to Him with a thankful heart.

Who is talking?

Beloved, believe not every spirit, but try the spirits
whether they are of God: because many false
prophets are gone out into the world. Hereby know
yea the Spirit of God: Every spirit that confesses that
Jesus Christ is come in the flesh is of God:

(1 John 4:1-2)

How do we know we are hearing from God and not
the devil or just talking to ourselves?

Best way I know is to look at what you are hearing
and ask yourself

- *Is this good for me – is this good for others?*
- *Is this going to hurt anyone?*
- *Is this full of love?*
- *Does this bring glory and honour to God's Holy Name*

God does not bring condemnation, guilt or pressure when
He speaks. He brings encouragement, direction and love.

Beloved, let us love one another: for love is of God;
and every one that love is born of God, and know God.

(1 John 4:7)

(*Always remember* the devil will never tell you he loves you and he will never want any good to come out of your prayer life.)

♦ Ask does what is being said line up with the Word of God?

Always go to the scriptures and see what the Word has to say.

If you are still not sure ask God for confirmation. This can be a word from someone you trust but had no knowledge of what you needed or you can do as Gideon did – he laid out what conclusion he wanted in order to confirm the rightness of the word of action he had received from the angel.

Gideon asked God to prove he was hearing correctly three times.

".. look, I will place a wool fleece on the threshing floor. If there is dew only on the fleece and all the ground is dry, then I will know that you will save Israel by my hand, as you said."

And that is what happened. Gideon rose early the next day; he squeezed the fleece and wrung out the dew—a bowlful of water.

(Judges 6:37-38).

The Holy Spirit in us does not condemn us or make us feel guilty either; His job is to challenge us to check our heart attitudes to ensure that we are on track in our relationships with God and with others.

What do we do when other people pray for us?

Just as there are different types of prayers there are different ways for people to pray with us and for us. Friends and family might offer to pray for us while we are together or from a distance, for example they could say '*I will pray for you while you are at school or at work.*'

Some people may want to hold your hands or touch your arms while they pray. If you feel comfortable with this then that is alright. However you need to be aware that *you do not have to let* everyone who offers to pray for you touch you when they pray.

> Paul went in to him and prayed, and he laid his hands on him, and healed him.

> (Acts 28:8)

Note: When Paul prayed it was *the Holy Spirit in Paul* who healed the man– not Paul himself.

In Christianity the act of *laying on of hands* is a prayerful impartation of spiritual power and/or the impartation of a spiritual calling from one person to another.

Only God knows the condition of a person's heart and spirit. No two people experience the world in the same way. People can often *look* and *sound* ok but they may be harbouring feelings of hurt in their hearts and in their spirits.

This does not mean that they will impart hurt to you because God protects you when you open yourself up to prayed for by others. *But* it could mean that their prayers may be influenced by their own hurtful experiences. If in doubt about the person or the prayer go to the scriptures and allow God's Word to confirm the truth of the prayer for you.

I would suggest that unless you know the person it could be best to say, *No thanks, my family prays with me.*'

Remember - when praying, and believing God is encouraging you to lay-hands on a person, *always* ask the person you are praying for if it is ok to touch them. If the person says it is ok *only ever* touch the person on the *arms* and *shoulders*. When you do this you are not being intrusive or invading the personal space of the other person.

At times you may be in church and you feel the minister has written his sermon just for you, when he calls for people to come forward for prayer you may decide to go out to the altar so that one of the ministry people can pray with. When you go out stand quietly and while you wait for someone to come and stand with you,

As in stranger danger – if it does not feel right to have someone praying for you – say so by telling them *'No thank you, I don't want prayer just now'*

You are allowed to say *'No Thank you'* to someone who offers to pray with you. This does not mean you are rejecting the Lord or what He is able to do for you and with you; it just means you are being careful about who speaks into your life.

The Holy Spirit in you will help you in this area of accepting prayer from people you do not know. Listen to Him- He will guide you, if you let Him.

What you can do when you are being prayed for by your parents, or a friend or someone in your Church group

- You may want to close your eyes and focus on what is being said.
- You may want to quietly agree with the prayer by softly speaking in tongues or simply saying "Yes Lord' or 'Thank you Father' or 'Thank you Jesus". When you agree in prayer it means you are open to receiving what is being spoken in the physical and the spirt.

There may be times when the Holy Spirit encourages you to stand silently and receive the words of the Lord being spoken to you.

- You might stand with your hands out stretched or simply hold them by your side.
- You might hold your hands in front of you as though you are catching the gift being given
- You might cry because of the Lord is healing a hurt in your heart or body.
- You might smile, or even laugh softly. because of the joy and beauty of God in your life

No two people are the same, so no two people will reach out for, or receive prayer in the same way. The person beside you may be laughing or crying or have fallen down, this does not mean that you have to do the same thing. You may be moved to laugh, cry or fall down but only do it if the Holy Spirit is moving you not because someone else did it. God made us all different.

When in a prayer line respect the opportunity for others to hear and receive prayer.

You do this by quietly seeking God yourself while you wait or by softly praying in agreement for other people receiving prayer. This is an excellent time to pray in tongues so that you are able to agree with what the Holy Spirit is doing in other people.

In our life-time many people will pray with us, and many people will speak words of prophecy and words of knowledge into our life. Not everything we hear will be God inspired but may be something spoken out of the speaker's good intentions.

Remember don't *just blindly accept* what is said to you *always* take it to the Lord and ask Him *'is this of you Lord?'*Read the scriptures and let God's Word show you the truth of the prayer you have received.

Are there wrong ways of praying?

Yes there are. Wrong Prayers *do not* bring glory to God's name.

- Wrong prayers *are selfish self-serving prayers* where you just want to get the better of someone else.
- Wrong prayers can be when we ask God to only bless people in limited ways.
- Wrong prayers *are when we tell God* how things should be done to help either ourselves or someone else without giving Him the freedom to decide how the situation can best bless everyone concerned.
- Wrong prayers *are when we ask God to punish someone because we think the person deserves to suffe*r. Maybe someone hurt us or acted unfairly against us, maybe they stole from us or caused us, and our family and friends, physical and emotional pain. We think the other person, in our eyes, really deserves to know how it feels to be hurt but it is not for us to call God's judgement or hurt upon them.

This is praying in a wrong heart attitude, praying from a place of turmoil in our heads and our hearts; this type of prayer is not asking God to bring good out of bad so that people can see God is good and loves us.

These prayers could be called word curses or evil assignments sent forth to bring harm to the person. And just as we can say them about some else they too can speak the same over us.

Don't fear these curses because *Jesus* gave us a way to live free of such things. We do this by breaking their power in the name of Jesus by binding all curses and assignments set by the evil one against you and your family and loose them back to the pit from where they came. Then we claim the promise of Jesus for our own

> "I will give you the keys of the kingdom of heaven; whatever you bind on earth will be bound in heaven, and whatever you loose on earth will be loosed in heaven"
>
> (Matthew 16:19, NIV).

- Wrong prayers can also be prayers prayed asking God to do something for someone so fervently that we forget to include God's Will in it. *God knows best*, He knows what is good for that person; for us all.

Our prayers and our Intercession should *always*, and *only*, ask for, and desire, God's Grace, Mercy and good Will for the people we pray for. *So when we pray*, after we pray what is on our hearts, our prayers should *end as Jesus' prayer did in the garden of Gethsemane,* with *but Father not my will but yours be done.*

Fasting and Praying

There are times you may be praying for something when the Lord may put it upon your heart to offer up a fast during this time of prayer. A fast can be from food or something you enjoy doing ie using the internet, watching TV, texting.

The Bible teaches us fasting and prayer break the yoke of bondage and brings about a release of God's presence, power, and provision into our lives.

Teachings on prayer and fasting in the Bible:

♦ Jesus did not require fasting as a part of Christianity:

"They [Pharisees] said to him, 'John's disciples often fast and pray, and so do the disciples of the Pharisees, but yours go on eating and drinking.' Jesus answered, 'Can you make the guests of the bridegroom fast while he is with them? But the time will come when the bridegroom will be taken from them; in those days they will fast.'"

♦ Fasting is a personal event:

"When you fast, do not look sombre as the hypocrites do, for they disfigure their faces to show men they are fasting. I tell you the truth; they have received their reward in full. But when you fast, put oil on your head and wash your face, so that it will not be obvious to men that you are fasting, but only to your Father, who is unseen; and your Father, who sees what is done in secret, will reward you"

(Matthew 6:16-18).

◆ Fasting is a form of worship:

"Then was a widow until she was eighty-four. She never left the temple but worshiped night and day, fasting and praying"

(Luke 2:37).

Here are a couple of other things that fasting can represent:

◆ Fasting allows you to offer up a sacrifice of something you enjoy for a period of time. The abstinence of something you enjoy is a way to show you are committed to praying and pushing through a spiritual blockage to get a breakthrough in the situation or in the area of your life you are seeking to grow in.
◆ Fasting can also bring you into a place of humbleness and openness so that the Lord is more able to work

without your natural nature resisting His touch in your heart and mind.

◆ Fasting in a corporate way – with the body of the church – brings a unity of purpose and a desire to allow the Lord work on a bigger scale – God loves it when his people stand together with one mind and one heart seeking Him with purpose and love, expecting Him to move.

Do you find...

...it is hard to ignore how others speak around you.

...it is so easy to fall into the trap of using their language to *fit in*.

Maybe you have never considered that you are able to change the atmosphere and the environment around you.

Maybe you have even left a place of work because you could not stand the way people around you joked and talked.

Have you ever thought it could be just as easy for others to fall into the way you act and the way you talk?

Some Types of Prayer

These are not the only types of prayer but just a selection of ways we are able to stand with our God for the concerns and needs of people and the world.

Thanking and praising God

God loves it when we come to Him in praise and thanks giving – in this way we acknowledge who He is and we give Him thanks for all He is doing and has done for us, for our family and friends, our school, our church and our country.

> Shout for joy to the Lord, all the earth. Worship the Lord with gladness; come before him with joyful songs.
>
> (Psalm 100v1-2)

Inviting God into our everyday life

God loves it when we come to Him with a good heart attitude (which is one open and loving Him and only wanting the best for everyone) and ask Him to be in the everyday things of our lives.

Seeking healing for ourselves

I have found that people have a tendency to look out for others but to put their own pain and problems on the back-burner as something to do something about sometime. God hates it when we are hurt or upset and He wants us to go to Him with the things that hurt us, take the things that upset us, to Him and ask Him to help make it better.

Seeking healing and help for others

God is pleased when we go to Him and ask Him to help our family and friends when they are not well or are worried about something.

Prayer of Protection

We are protected by the Blood of Jesus. Have you ever heard the song "There is power, power miracle working power in the blood, in the blood of Jesus"?

Well it's true. Jesus died so that we might live. When His blood was shed on the cross for us it became the power of our salvation. His blood was shed to save us and protect us from sin in life and hell in death.

When we take Communion we are asked to do so in remembrance of Jesus. What are we remembering? We are remembering the power of the blood shed for us on the cross. It not only redeemed us from a life of sin; it was shed to protect us from the temptation to sin against God and each other; it was shed to save us from an eternity in darkness and damnation. *So in faith, and with authority, we use its power to defeat the enemy by declaring the protection of the Blood of Jesus all over us.*

When the enemy uses his only weapons – lies and deception – whispers fear and doubt into our minds we must stand firm and declare that we are children of the Most High God and we under the protection of the Blood of Jesus shed for us and all those we are praying for.

Repentance and Forgiveness

God waits for us to run to Him when:
- something goes wrong
- we do something wrong
- we say something bad
- we think something wrong

God does not want us to be like Adam and Eve, He does not want us to sin and then hide from Him in the hope that He did not see.

Of course He saw what you did, but it is not about Him knowing you did something wrong it is about us choosing to go to Him; confessing that we knew it was not the right thing to do and asking Him to forgive us and to help us do better next time.

God loves us as much as He ever will, right now. There is absolutely nothing you can do that will ever make Him love you more than He does right now. *And* there is absolutely nothing you can do that will ever make Him love you less than He does *this very moment.*

His Grace and Mercy is always there for us – we have only to go to Him.

Another type of prayer is the prayer of a Christian warrior.

Prayers of Warfare

"The weapons we fight with are not the weapons of the world. On the contrary, they have divine power to demolish strongholds. We demolish arguments and every pretension that sets itself up against the knowledge of God, and we take captive every thought to make it obedient to Christ."

(2 Corinthians 10:4-5)

Who is a warrior? I am – You are

When we accepted Jesus into our heart and became a child of God, we also became a fighter for the Kingdom of God and committed to sharing the Good News of Jesus.

This means we need to know God has already prepared a way. We are battle ready when we know the power of the Holy Spirit who dwells in us. *Ephesians6:10-18* tells us that the battle we fight is not physical but one where the evil one will try to attack our hearts and our thoughts.

It is at these times when you will need to put on the armour of God and stand firm against these attacks. *These attacks can be subtle* – like when you might be feeling sick or a bit sad or thinking your friends don't like you– *Or They can be very obvious*– like when you are being disagreeable or when people around you are fighting and being nasty.

This is the time to stand against strife and time to declare God's victory.

When we stand with Jesus with a heart attitude to see the victory then we are able *to go in and defeat the enemy and his plans to hurt us by speaking the Word of God* and telling the devil to '*go in Jesus Name!*'

Ephesians 6v10-18 - Tells of the armour of God and that the battle is in the spiritual realm so we are to put on the armour and stand firm in our faith.

- The belt of truth is the Word of God which is to be wrapped around us and securely held in our hearts
- The breastplate of righteousness – protects our heart
- We are to stand on the Word of God – knowing its truth
- We are to take up the shield of faith which deflects all the arrows of the evil one – We are then to stand fast believing that God is God and He is able to do all things and He always bring good out of every situation and circumstance in our lives to His Glory.
- The helmet of salvation – protects our mind and thoughts from the lies and deceit of the evil one.
- Take up the sword of the Spirit and speak the Word of God into the situation, cutting through any evil plan that has been devised to:
  - stop us knowing and loving God
  - stop us telling others of the love of God for them

◆   And lastly we are encouraged to pray in tongues –
    which is the language of the Spirit – holding fast to
    our belief and trust in Jesus.

We are to remember God always has our back – in
all things. He never leaves us to fight a battle alone.
We have the Holy Spirit and an army of Angels with
us always.

> Now when the attendant of the man of God had
> risen early and gone out, behold, an army with
> horses and chariots was circling the city. And his
> servant said to him, "Alas, my master! What shall we
> do?" So he answered, "Do not fear, for those who
> are with us are more than those who are with them."
>
> Then Elisha prayed and said, "O Lord, I pray, open
> his eyes that he may see." And the Lord opened
> the servant's eyes, and he saw; and behold, the
> mountain was full of horses and chariots of fire
> all around Elisha.
>
> (Isaiah 6:15-17)

God's people need two things if they are going to
appropriate God's resources against the enemy and
experience God's deliverance. They need *eyes to see* the
mighty power and provision of God, but they must also
believe God and put on their God-given armour that they
might, with confidence, take a stand against Satan and
his forces.

Sometimes I act out putting on the armour of God because the very act of dressing in it reminds me that, even though I am putting on spiritual armour, it is still very real. I pretend it is all set out on a chair and:

- I will pick up the Belt of Truth and tie it round my waist
- I will put my arms through the straps of the Breastplate of Righteousness and buckle them tightly
- I will stand on God's promises of protection and provision
- I will pick up the Shield of Faith and slide my arm into the fitting to hold it firm
- I will lift the Helmet of Salvation onto my head and tighten the chin strap
- I pick up the Sword of the Spirit and know that the Word of God is as sharp as a two edged sword and cuts both ways. There is never a time when the Word of God does not cut through the fog of lies and deceit woven into our hearts and minds by the evil one.
- Then I lift my voice calling out my readiness and honouring God in the language we share.

If God is able to do all things you might ask ...

Why does He need me to do anything? The answer is He doesn't.

But – and this is a big *but*– God Loves us so much He wants us to be active in building a friendship with Him, so He invites too share the victory of the Cross with Him. God wants us to know Him as He knows us.

Binding and Loosening

This type of prayer is good when we feel something *'yuck'* around us. We are able to use our God given authority and tell all ungodly things that 'we bind them and loose them away from us in Jesus name'.

Quote scripture, say for it is written in Matthew 18v18…

> Jesus said "I tell you the truth, whatever you bind on earth will be bound in heaven, and whatever you loose on earth will be loosed in heaven."
>
> (Matthew 18:18)

Don't be polite, evil is not polite to you, just tell the Devil and all his dark angels to go back to the pit of hell from where they came.

They have no right to bother you. Jesus defeated them. He took away any power they thought they had over Him and His disciples. You are His disciple; therefore they have no power over you or your family and must go away when we speak with the authority Jesus gave to us.

Remember We are strong in Jesus and able to stand our ground and defeat the evil one as he comes against us or our family and friends.

> "I can do all things in Christ Jesus who strengthens me"
>
> (Philippians 4v13)

However we are encouraged by Jesus not to be 'lone rangers', we don't have to stand alone.

"...where two or more stand together in My name..."
(Matthew 18v20)

What does this mean 'To Bind and Loosen'?

Imagine wrapping something up so tightly in plastic; then in rope and in chains – now you have bound it so tightly; it cannot move; it cannot breathe.

Imagine dipping it in liquid nitrogen – where it freezes and becomes brittle – now imagine hitting it with a hammer and smashing it into a thousand million little bits that can never be pieced together again.

This is what happens when we bind and loosen in the name of Jesus. Demons and their plans to deceive us are destroyed because

We are of God...and...greater is he that is in you,
than he that is in the world.

(1 John 4:4)

Cleansing prayer

Why do we pray this type of prayer?

Have you ever owned a puppy you bathed and flea powdered regularly to ensure she had no fleas. Then you take her for a walk only to come home and have her scratch because somewhere she has mixed with other dogs that do have fleas and some of them have jumped onto her.

How do you clean her? You take her home and wash her afresh.

This is what can happen to us as we go about our day. We can be washed fresh and under the protection of the blood of Jesus; we can be filled with the Holy Spirit as we leave home but during the day things do not go as well as they should and we let our guard down –just a little.

Then things can start to annoy and frustrate us and before we know it, other people are bugging us! Then we may say and/or do things that are not good for us or those around us. We have picked up other people's *fleas*.

How can we cleanse ourselves when these niggles start?

For me, I run to the scriptures. I put on the armour of God and I take up the two edged sword of the Spirit. Then I speak with the authority given to me through Jesus – I cut off all hard, harsh and ungodly words spoken by me, to me or about me, and I speak a fresh washing of the blood of Jesus over me. The word of God tells us that by His blood we are washed clean and made acceptable unto Him.

> …just as Christ loved the church (we are the church). He gave up his life for her to make her holy and clean, washed by the cleansing of God's word.
>
> (Ephesians 5:26 NLT)

We need to be ever vigilant to the small things around us because the devil is a deceiver and will try to creep up on us to make the small irritating things of our life into big over-powering problems before we even realise it.

> Your enemy the devil prowls around like a roaring lion looking for someone to devour.
>
> (1 Peter 5:8)

Silent Prayer

(from Psalm 46:10)

This type of prayer time is a time when you wait on God to speak.

It is a time when *you stop talking* and *sit quietly in God's presence* and wait on Him.

When you don't know what to pray, either in a group or as a single person, this is a good starting point.

Stop and offer up to God a time of silence and wait to hear what is on His heart.

- Sometimes He will give you pictures or visions of what is on His heart
- Sometimes He will drop a word into your heart
- Sometimes He will just tell you how much He loves you.
- Sometimes you may not hear a word you may simply be washed in a sense of peace and goodwill as God pours out His love for you.
- Sometimes you may put on some worship music to softly play in the background and your silent time may be as simple as sitting in a comfortable chair,

or lying down, closing your eyes and listening to the music and words of the song.

◆ Sometimes you may fall into a peaceful sleep and this is ok as well for the Lord does not stop enjoying your company and speaking to your spirit just because your physical body rests.

Set a time limit if you need to but remember when you offer up a time of silent prayer, do not be in a hurry – there are times when your whole prayer tim\e might be just sitting with God.

There is a healing to be found in being silent before God.

> The Lord is my shepherd, I lack nothing. He
> makes me lie down in green pastures, He leads
> me beside quiet waters, He refreshes my soul.
>
> (Psalm 23:1-3)

All prayer is important to the Lord but for me this type of praying is special as it gives God the opportunity to lead my heart and my thoughts so that they become in-tune with His.

When we stand in faith and call on the name of Jesus – the evil one and his demonic forces become confused and disorientated because suddenly the person they are annoying, the person they are trying to make angry, has disappeared and there before them stands the image of Jesus.

If you can think of a can of flea-spray we use to put an invisible shield between our dogs and the fleas. It is the same when we know Jesus in our lives we have an invisible shield of protection around us forever.

Structured Prayer

Sometimes you may be led by the Holy Spirit to pray prayers over a period of time until you get the breakthrough you are looking for.

You may find it helpful at these times to have the prayers written down so that you are able to stay on track with your prayers.

These written guidelines may include verses or whole chapters to read aloud.

As a young Christian, I carried with me a written prayer to help me learn how to pray in faith and stand firm before adversity – this did not make the prayer any less real or powerful because I was praying from the heart and believing the devil had no right to be in my face. I used this tool of a written prayer, with scriptures, to help me learn how to speak with the authority within me that comes from Jesus.

Reading bible verses, Psalms and Proverbs is a powerful tool for *no* Word of the Lord ever returns void and the devil has to flee before the Word of the Lord.

"...so is my word that goes out from my
mouth: It will not return to me empty, but will
accomplish what I desire and achieve the purpose
for which I sent it."

(Isaiah 55:11)

Some churches have times of corporate prayer. *(Corporate prayer is when everyone prays one prayer point at a time in a group).*

Some churches have prayer led by the Minister or Priest. At these times the Priest or Minister or Pastor will pray and invite the congregation to respond with a set response. *For example* – the minister might pray a prayer over the people and end with "*God be with you*' and the people will reply *"and also with you"* or something similar.

God hears and answers all prayer – He may not answer in the way we expect. We must remember to pray with the understanding that *God's answer could be anyone of three answers. Yes, No, Maybe.* We have to trust His reply will always be the best one for us at that time.

God hears not only the words being spoken but He also looks into the heart of the person praying. So ask the Lord to check your heart, so whether you are reading a written prayer, praying in a group or praying as an individual you will be talking to God with a heart praying for the best for the person and the situation you are taking to Him.

Prayer should always only want the best for everyone.

Why does the evil one have to flee?

Because when Jesus came to fulfil Old Testament prophesy and provide us a way to reconcile with God, He took away every weapon Satan had over mankind. Satan was left powerless and we, His sons and daughters, were armed!

> And having disarmed the powers and authorities,
> he made a public spectacle of them, triumphing
> over them by the cross.
>
> (Colossians 2v15)

He took back any right the devil had to torment us – Jesus took back the keys to the kingdom and opened a way for us to stand against the deception whispered by the evil one. Jesus left him with nothing but the power to whisper untruths into our ears in the hope that we will believe them. When we say – *be gone from here in Jesus name* Satan trembles because he remembers the last time Jesus fought him.

Spiritual Power Tool - Anointing with Oil

In the Bible "anointing with Holy Oil" means to make sacred, to consecrate or to set apart, and dedicate it for use unto our *Creator*.

There are three types of Anointing for people: Sacred, medical and ordinary.

The Apostle John writes in 1John 2:27, *that anointing refers to a Sacred spiritual process in which the Holy Spirit empowers a person's heart and mind with Yahweh's truth and love.*

The Apostle's went out two by two...and anointed the sick (Ps.23:5; Mar.6:13). Elders of the church are instructed to anoint the sick for the purpose of healing (Jam.5:14). The dead are anointed before burial (Mar.14:3-9)

The Prophet Isaiah writes 10:27, "*...the yoke [of the evil one] will be destroyed because of the anointing oil.*" You can anoint yourself by taking some oil and place a small amount on your forehead and claim *Yahweh's* promise of *His* strength (Ps.92:10).

One thing I have discovered is that *it does not need to be oil.* When I am open to anoint, consecrate, dedicate something/ someone for God I take some water; I dedicate the water to God by thanking Him for the water and ask Him to make acceptable it unto Him to be used to anoint for His Glory.

Oil is good because it matches with the Word of the Lord, *but* sometimes there just isn't any oil in the cupboard, the car or at the beach when God speaks to my heart and says pray and 'anoint this person for Me'.

What do I do?

I use what is at hand because *it is not about the liquid I use - it is about obeying, honouring and glorifying God.*

Prayer can be like talking to a Friend on the phone

When you talk to your friend over the telephone how do you know what they are saying?
- Do you both talk at the same time?
- Do you try and drown them out by talking louder because it is only your words that are important?
- Do you get to the end of the call and wonder what on earth was said?
- Do you hesitate in calling your friend because you do not feel you are being heard?

Or

- Do you take it in turns talking, giving each other the opportunity to share your ideas and thoughts?
- Do you take the time to listen to what your friend has to say, and give value to your friend's words?
- Do you hear when they are upset and give them comfort and encouragement?
- Do you hear their happiness when something good happens and share their delight?
- Do you offer words of wisdom into difficult situations?
- Do you tell them you are excited to have them as a friend?
- *God* wants to talk with you like you want to talk to your friend on the phone.

Do you think you could give it a go?

The best time to talk to God is when you do not want to.

Things in your life go wrong:
- someone crashes into your car and your insurance policy doesn't over the cost of the hire car
- all your bills turn up at once which is just fine until suddenly you have an emergency and need cash

The list can go on forever. And it is so easy to sit and think "What's the use? I do everything I am supposed to do but it is just no good. Everything is falling apart."

And so you stop talking to God; and the devil wins because he hates it when you talk to God.

So when things are hard and you feel like there is no hope, no way out of the quagmire you are in GO TO GOD.
- Tell Him you feel discarded, rejected, and alone
- Tell Him it is all just too hard to do
- Tell Him how you feel.

BE REAL with Him because you may not see any way out of the mess you are in but he does. Just talk to Him and keep on talking to him.

When we talk to God about our sad and hard times then we are praying and surrendering our independence and asking Him to give us His Strength, His Wisdom and His Will to find a way through the situation.

Just talk to Him.

Humble yourself before the Lord

"If my people, who are called by my name, will humble themselves and pray and seek my face and turn from their wicked ways, then will I hear from heaven and will forgive their sins and will heal their land."

(2 Chronicles 7:14)

P*owerful, sobering, promising words.*

This is your Father. If you do not approach him as a humble little child would approach his father for help, then do you really want his help?

(Luke 18:17)

How can you humble yourself? *Just be honest with God.* Talk to him about how you are feeling, tell him what you are thinking

God already knows what is in your heart and in your head.

But to be humble before the Lord is to be vulnerable. To be vulnerable is to expose your inner most thoughts and feelings, expose every good and bad thing about you.

In our lives we put up barriers in our hearts, to stop the world from hurting us in our inner most thoughts and feelings. Because we know people are not always kind we protect ourselves.

God does not want us to come with our heart safe behind a barrier of hardness and built up hurt.

When we are open and vulnerable to God we are in a place of trust knowing that He knows us, every part of us, and He loves and accepts us just as we are. Nothing we do is a surprise to Him. He knew us before we were born and He knows us now.

He wants to have a relationship, a friendship, where we trust Him enough to tell him everything we do, think and say.

Praying from a place of humility means that you are seeking God to do the work and you may never know whether your prayers were answered or not.

An important thing about prayer is that *you don't need to know* how your prayer was answered. That is between God and the person who needed the prayer.

Private prayer alone with God is very precious to Him. As a matter of fact, Jesus condemned public, prideful prayer:

> And when you pray, do not be like the hypocrites, for they love to pray standing in the synagogues and on the street corners to be seen by men. I tell you the truth; they have received their reward in full.
>
> (Matthew 6:5)

Falling down or 'being slain in the spirit

When people are being prayed for sometimes the Holy Spirit fills them and they simply trust Him enough to give over their bodies to Him – and they fall to the ground allowing Him to complete the work that He has begun.

> "... that then the house was filled with a cloud, even the house of the Lord; so that the priests could not stand to minister by reason of the cloud; for the glory of the Lord had filled the house of God."

> (2 Chronicles 5:14)

This is not a *must* – this is an offering of trust – a denying the opinion of man, because if you felt the soft touch of the Holy Spirit and you lost strength in your legs and started to collapse then the devil would want to say *'you look silly. You are being foolish? Your friends are laughing at you – look at them can't you see them laughing?'*

The evil one's plan is to take your focus off the Lord God and get you to worry about what people might think of you. When you listen to him, he wins because he has stopped you hearing the truth God is speaking into your life.

You always have the choice– whether to accept what God is doing or not. You can choose not to let the Holy Spirit move you and stand or you can offer your whole self and be open to falling to the floor. Either way the Lord will speak to you. *You don't lose or disappoint God it is just a choice.*

God gave us the freedom to choose. This is not to say you will Fall down every time you are prayed for. Sometimes the Lord will speak and touch your heart and life and you will not have the urge to fall down. And this is OK too.

We are to be led by the Holy Spirit in these things. There is a time and a place for all these things and we need to be mindful that it is the Holy Spirit leading us to laugh, cry or fall down.

Warning we are *not to 'play'* at any of these things. We are not to laugh just to be seen to be laughing.

We are not to cry just to be seen to be crying.

And we are not to fall down just because we think we need to be seen to be falling down in order to let others think that the Spirit of God touched our lives.

The Lord wants a heart that is able to genuinely move with the Spirit – not one that pretends so that other people will think we are close with the Lord.

Be real with God. Treat your relationship with Him as special. Don't use it to impress your friends or mock the Holy Spirit who dwells in you.

Do you believe that one person can make a difference?

I do. One person with Jesus on their side can change the world.

How? Pray.

Before you go out of the house take a moment and pray.

Ask the Lord God to go before you into the day and touch the hearts, lips and minds of all whom you will deal with?

Before you enter your work place take a moment and pray.

Dedicate it and all it stands for to the Lord God. Ask Him to go before you and to prepare the hearts and the minds of all your colleagues to be receptive to the gentle touch of the Holy Spirit, ask the Holy Spirit to guide your own thoughts words and actions so that you may glorify the Lord God this day in this place for His name's sake.

As the advertisement says – it may not happen overnight but it will happen.

Our God is a God of all possibilities and He is able to change your environment if you are willing to stand with Him for the salvation of all you meet.

The reason we should want our environments to be 'nicer' to work in is because we want everyone around us to know the kindness of Jesus flowing out of their hearts. We should want, with Jesus the salvation of everyone we know, and their families and friends.

How can we get there? One step at a time – One prayer at a time.

The Name of Jesus

When we are go to school we discover there are times when the school will need parents to do things to help out for fundraising or clean-up teams– a letter may go home asking for help and our mum or dad may ask you to put their name down to help.

When they do this they give you the authority to use their name and commit them to helping out. They then back you up by turning up and helping the school.

The Holy Bible tells us God gave His authority to Jesus to tell the people of His love, to tell demons and devils to get out of people's lives, to heal the sick and to bring dead people back to life. God gave Jesus, His authority over life and dead.

> When he had said this, Jesus called in a loud voice, "Lazarus, come out!" The dead man came out, his hands and feet wrapped with strips of linen, and a cloth around his face.
>
> (John 11v43-44)

When we accepted who Jesus is – Son of the One True Living God – and what He did for us – died in our place on the cross – redeemed us from our life of sin and healed all of our illnesses. We became sons and daughters of *God* and in doing so we were also given the authority to go into the world and do what Jesus did.

> … Finally Paul … turned around and said to the spirit, "In the name of Jesus Christ I command you to come out of her!" At that moment the spirit left her.
>
> (Acts 16v17-18)

Not only were we given the authority of a child to speak the Father's name we were given the power of the Holy Spirit to heal the sick and move impossible obstacles through faith.

> Jesus said"…I tell you the truth, if you have faith as small as a mustard seed, you can say to this mountain, 'Move from here to there' and it will move. Nothing will be impossible for you"
>
> (Matthew 17:20).

People who lived under the Old Testament where so afraid of misusing the Name of God they would not name Him outside of times of prayer and blessing.

Today the name of Jesus is misused by many people. Sometimes people
- use His name as a curse and yell *'Jesus Christ'*
- whisper it when they are scared *'Jesus Christ'*
- are exasperated and say *'Jesus'*

- shortened His name to '*Jeez*' or '*Christ*' and use it when they are angry
- people also abuse the name of the Holy Spirit by saying '*Holy Ghost*'
- bring God's name into their conversations by saying '*Oh My God*'
- or texting or saying 'OMG' just to express themselves.

People saying these things may think we are mad for not using these terminologies in our everyday speech

But

Honouring the Name of God was so important to God it was one of the first things to be recorded in the Bible.

"You shall not take the name of the Lord your God in vain, for the Lord will not leave him unpunished who takes His name in vain."

(Exodus 20:7)

God's Name – Jesus' Name – the Name of the Holy Spirit is filled with the power to change our lives, to bring about changes in our world.

- God created the heavens and the earth and all life on it
- Jesus cast out demons and healed the sick
- The Holy Spirit raised Jesus from the dead

Jesus is your friend, so don't misuse His name or throw it about like He won't care. Jesus does care how you handle His name. He wants you to care too.

Keep His name as something special – because it is special, demons flee at the mention of His *Name*.

Our God is the Creator of Heaven and Earth.

- He is the God of abundance.
- He is able to do things we think are impossible.
- He is the God of healing and health.

His name should not be used to express surprise, or anger or frustration or as a swear word. I encourage you to honour the Lord's Name and keep it close to your heart and encourage others to do the same.

Jesus and the Holy Spirit in us

God sent His Son so that we could hear of His love.

'God so loved the world he gave his own son so
that all who accept Him may have eternal life'.

(John 3:16)

Jesus came so that we would have a way to know and love God.

Jesus came so that we would be able to build a relationship with God.

Jesus came and exposed all the lies of the enemy.

Jesus did not leave us to walk, talk or live alone. He knew, and God knew we, as humans would be surrounded by temptations. Knew we would need to be encouraged and guided every day of our lives. Guided to choose good over evil, guided to choose to accept other people for who they are; guided to pray for ourselves and for others.

Jesus prayed for his friends and family – we can too.

"…Christ Jesus is He who died, yes, rather who
was raised, who is at the right hand of God, who
also intercedes for us…"

(Romans 8v34)

We have *the gift of the Holy Spirit* living in us to help us know and love God more. We have the Holy Spirit to guide us and help us choose to do things God's way.

> And I will pray the Father, and he shall give you another Comforter, that he may abide with you for ever;
>
> (John 14:16)

> But the Comforter, which is the Holy Ghost, whom the Father will send in my name, he shall teach you all things, and bring all things to your remembrance, whatsoever I have said unto you.
>
> (John 14:26)

> Nevertheless I tell you the truth; It is expedient for you that I go away: for if I go not away, the Comforter will not come unto you; but if I depart, I will send him unto you.
>
> (John 16:7)

We have the Holy Spirit speaking into our hearts the words of God and then taking our thoughts, prayers, words back to God's heart through the Love of Jesus. God loves us – God hungers to hear our thoughts and share our days – God sent His *Holy Spirit* to dwell with in us all the days of our lives. God loves it when we talk to Him. How do we know this? – He tells us in His written word.

In the same way the Spirit also helps our weakness; for we do not know how to pray as we should, but the Spirit Himself intercedes for us with wordless groans. And he who searches our hearts knows the mind of the Spirit, because the Spirit intercedes for God's people in accordance with the will of God.

(Romans 8v26-27)

Receiving an Answer

It is all very well to pray for ourselves and have others pray for us *but* unless we actually decide to receive the answer we will be back praying the same things over and over again.

After you pray stop a moment and give yourself the opportunity to:
- *Receive* God's Answer/guidance
- *Receive* God's Forgiveness
- *Receive* God's Healing
- *Receive* God's Love and Peace
- *Receive* God's blessings

Then, by faith, receive by simply saying "Thank you Lord I willingly receive from You'.

Guidelines for People who pray

Praying aloud was scary for me. I had never prayed out loud in a group and I had no idea of what to do or what was expected of me.

I realised that if I felt this way then the people I was about to pray with might also be wondering how to behave and what to do in the group environment.

What I did not expect was to discover that these guidelines for praying in the group would become a powerful tool in helping me in my own prayer life.

The following format and rules on prayer etiquette helped me to understand it is essential for people who pray to feel they are in a 'safe zone'.

- Approach prayer time with a thankful heart full of songs, praising God – and honouring Him.
- After this worship time share who and what is on our hearts to pray about.
- To keep focused, and to remember requests, make a list of prayer requests either on a notepad or on a whiteboard.
- Before praying for these requests take a few minutes to be silent to wait on God so that He is able to share what He has on His heart to pray for.

- After a few minutes share what the Lord had shown you, and add this to the group's prayer list.
- Use a *Prayer Tool* (a small bean bag or a ball is good), the person holding the tool is to be the one praying out loud while everyone else prays silently in agreement.
- Unless previously arranged the first person to pray might indicate their willingness by asking for the prayer tool. If two or more called for the tool then the co-ordinator of the group could indicate the order in which to pray.

(E.g. Sally held the prayer tool while she opened in prayer then passed it to Joe on her right, who then passed it James, etc.)

Trust

No teasing anyone about a prayer need – if we can't be open and honest within our prayer group then we lie to *God* while we protect ourselves because if we don't trust our prayer partners to honour our secret hopes, desires, needs how can we be honest about them.

For a prayer group to work *each* person needs to know that prayer requests are safe and will not be talked about as if they don't matter.

Confidentiality

Prayer requests are to be treated as something special and *are not* to be talked about just to share the information around–

we expose ourselves and become vulnerable when we ask for prayer because we are asking someone to stand with us as we talk to God about something very personal.

Prayer requests are not up for general conversation outside of prayer time.

If you are asked to support someone in prayer you *do not* gossip with others about the person or the need for prayer – You have been invited to be part of someone's private needs not given a piece of information to share around with everyone.

If you feel you would like someone else to pray with you - go to someone *you trust* – mum, dad, brother, sister or friend – and you might say

"I have a prayer request and would like you to stand with me while I lift it to the Lord".

Or

"…my friend John needs prayer for school" or "my friend Joan is having problems at home" or "there are problems at the swimming pool" or "I have a personal need just now; could you stand with me?"

This should be enough information to enable the person you trust to pray in agreement with you as you support your friend in prayer.

A Prayer Partner

A prayer partner should be someone who knows the Lord, and is willing to stand with you in your prayer needs.

A prayer partner should be someone you trust to be listening to and walking with God.

A prayer partner should just not talk about how God is working in their life but living a life showing the love of God to others.

A prayer partner should not need to know all the particulars of the problem to be able to stand with us in prayer.

Why?

Because God already knows the needs of the people we pray for – He already knows the circumstances surrounding them are in – He just want us to care enough to bring them to Him in prayer.

God wants to know if we love *Him* enough to love and pray for whoever and whatever situation He puts on our hearts.

And this is where true prayer comes from – remember the Intercession Circle

The prayer need comes from *God*

Who then asks the *Holy Spirit* to speak it into our hearts?

We then can pray about the need and *ask for God's help in Jesus' name*

Our prayers go to *Jesus* who gives them back to *God*

Everyone is Equal

God hears all prayer on an equal basis. No one prayer is better and another.

It doesn't matter whether it's the Minister or Pastor praying, our parents or the lady next to us – every prayer that is spoken, every prayer that is offered up to *God* is received by him as being important. He does not separate the prayers into urgent and non-urgent piles; to God all prayer is urgent because He knows how much the prayer matters to the person praying.

It doesn't matter whether the prayer comes from a person who has been a Christian 1 year, 50 years or whether a small child offers up the prayer, God rejoices because the prayer came.

For the Group - No one is to try to make anyone else in the group feel bad or tease them or joke about whether (in their opinion) the prayer was good or bad, long or short.

Everyone is different, everyone will pray differently to everyone else. That is the uniqueness of people. God did not make us to sound and act the same. God loves us because we are all different, love Him differently, talk to Him differently, and walk with Him differently. He does not want us to all sound and act the same as anyone else in the world.

Encourage one another

Praying out loud can be scary –because we all think that we won't get it right – not just children but adults too -

But the good thing about praying out loud is that *God* encourages us and we get better at it.

When praying within a group it is good to have some structure to allow everyone to feel safe enough to pray within the group.

- *Don't* make fun of how another person prays but rather pray in agreement and, in doing so, encourage the Holy Spirit to speak more so that we are then all encouraged to step out and pray what the Lord puts on our hearts.

- *Don't* tell the person praying you think they did it wrong – because maybe the way they prayed was exactly the way God wanted them to pray.

No prayer is wrong if, it is prayed in accordance with *God's will.* Sometimes we think that we know what to pray to fix the situation but it may not be the way that God wants it done right now

When we pray we have to trust God– trust Him to answer our prayers by providing the best solution for the person we are praying for.

God is bigger than any prayer we can ever pray – when we pray God's Will Be Done we recognise - that even if we got the pray need wrong or did something we think is unfixable - *God He is big enough to fix anything man has broken* – God wants us to invite Him into the situation and ask for His Will to be done.

No-one is better than anyone else – *some* of us have prayed out loud more than others *but that does not make our prayer any better* than anyone else's.

It just means that we have been brave enough to step outside our comfort zone of silent praying into a world where we express what is on our heart in a voice that others can hear. When we step out into the scary world of praying aloud, *God* encourages us to do it more and more because in this way we are able to encourage others to also pray out loud without feeling self-conscious. (Without being afraid of what others will say or think of the way we pray).

Short Sweet and Simple

Don't complicate your prayers with too many words.

When we stand and pray what *God* has put on our hearts then that prayer is good and it will be long enough to say what you need to say.

Some of us use different words. Say things differently – think about things different.

Some people pray long, loud prayers – some people pray soft, short prayers.

When you pray from an open heart wanting what God wants then there is no wrong way to pray.

The disciples approached Jesus about how to pray and he taught them what we know as the Lord's *Prayer*. This prayer calls out to God the Father, acknowledging how Great He is, humbling the person praying by acknowledging that without God we are nothing, reminds us of what God did for us.

He forgave us – and asks that we do the same, reminds us that He is able to protect us when we call on him and in return we give him all the glory.

For me I now know that when I pray the Lord's Prayer I pray in the Will of God. *But* as a new Christian I was concerned about not praying the right words or the right way or I was not following the right pattern– I felt the Lord say me to just *kiss* it Suzanne and it will be alright.

Keep It Simple Suzanne– so I pass this wisdom on to you as you start to pray – do not feel pressured to have big prayers, or loud prayers or the longest prayer, or try to cover everything in the world in one prayer but rather keep it simple and pray what God puts on your heart to say at that time.

One person at a time

In the group *every one* who wants to pray will have the opportunity to do so. There may be a time when we are all praying to the Lord at the same time. We will treat this time as semi-private and ask people to pray as though talking face to face with a friend, and not in a way to dominate the time with their own voice.

At other times *only* the person holding the prayer tool will be praying aloud. This will give each of participants the opportunity to grow in confidence in being able to pray to God.

Respect the person praying and don't pray so loudly that the person praying cannot be heard by everyone in the group.

You are able to support the person with the prayer tool by softly praying in agreement as God leads you. You will be encouraged to *not talk during prayer time -*

sometimes we talk, make noises just so people know we are there. Within our Prayer time you do not need to do this because *as the leader of the group.*

I see you. You are not forgotten nor are you invisible to me or the group.

I ask you to trust God will show me you are ready to pray.

I ask you to respect when others are praying and patiently wait your turn.

Respect

It is important to respect the person with the Prayer Tool by letting him/her pray without interruption. By allowing the other person time to pray we should receive the same respect when it is our turn to pray.

Respect God by trusting Him to give us the words to pray for the needs He *has placed on our hearts.*

When you pray with in a group, you may find your thoughts being filled with prayer needs other than the one being prayed about. This can lead to you being distracted in other ways by the enemy. You might suddenly be thinking about your school day, or the new toy you have, or a TV program that you want to watch.

And so, you stop thinking about God and why you are even praying.

This is not uncommon. It is a weapon used the enemy to discourage us from standing up with *God* to pray for a situation or a need.

To stop this distraction of the enemy *you must choose to bring your thoughts back* to where you are. You can do this by either praying quietly in tongues or quietly praying the Lord's Prayer so that God is able to help focus your thoughts allowing you to again be praying in unison with the rest of the group.

Please remember - The enemy knows *if* he can stop us praying – he wins – because when we stop praying we stop listening to *God*. The enemy's only plan is to rob, steal and destroy.

He wants *to steal our time with God*

He wants *to rob us of our joy in life*

He wants *to destroy our trust in, and friendship with God*

We *stop* the enemy's plans by:

Praying and talking to God,

Singing to God and

Thanking God for loving us

Respect the Right to say NO

Not everyone you offer to pray with will be open to your offer of prayer.

When you feel you would like to pray with someone, approach them with the offer of prayer. Give them the opportunity to choose.

For example you could say: *Would you like me to pray with you?*

Just as you have the right to refuse prayer *so does everyone else.* Just because you offer to pray *does not mean that the other person is obliged to let you pray.* They also have the right to say *No thank you.*

Do not take offence. This is not a rejection of you; it is simply the person asserting his or her right to choose whether or not he or she want to be prayed for at this time.

Be polite, excuse yourself, as you walk away silently thank the Lord that He will bless the person and meet every need they have. You can continue to pray for them as the Lord leads whenever He brings them to your thoughts.

Why Worship through Prayer and Intercession?

Because He first loved you, He cares for you, He cares about you, He is the best friend you will ever know, and He wants to share your life with you.

How can Prayer and Intercession be Worship?

Because praising and thanking God through bringing our needs, our family's needs, our friends' needs and the needs of the world to Him in prayer is allowing *His Name* to be *glorified* when our prayers are answered. Worshiping God is Glorifying God.

Prayer is Praising God by giving Him
- time and trust
- thoughts and dreams
- concerns and cares
- compassion
- ears to listen to Him and what He cares about
- a heart to feel His love
- eyes to see the beauty of all His creation
- a mouth to speak with
- tears of joy and tears of pain
- friendship

Intercession is thanking God for
- helping a friend
- helping your family
- healing the sick
- mending what is broken
- shining a light in a dark place
- helping to find your dog
- protecting you and your family
- providing for you and your family
- allowing you to stand with Him in prayer for all the lost, lonely, hurting people of the world
- protecting and helping all those who need him

BE HUMBLE in your faith walk
and your prayer growth

Every single person is an individual; which means that *no two faith walks are the same*. I have not experienced the same things in my life that you have so I will always look at life; look at God; look at other people differently to you. It is the same with my faith walk with God.

My faith walk is not, and will never be the same as yours. This does not mean that my faith is greater or lesser than your faith; it just means that it is different – we are different –we are individuals. God does not love any one person more than the other: He loves our individuality.

Why is this you may ask?
My answer to this question is simply because I needed different things from God in different ways to you.

It was only when God challenged me to teach the children of the church about Prayer and Intercession that I realised He had given me a different perspective to other people, different insights that other people had not yet asked for.

I humbly offer up this, My Notebook on Prayer and Intercession, in the hope that you, the reader will be able to gather a greater understanding of God's heart desire to share everything in your life through the communion of prayer.

There is power in the Name of Jesus

When you don't know how to pray, or what to say speak the name of *'Jesus'*.

When you ae in danger and you only have time to say *one word* – make that word *Jesus*.

He will hear you.

He is the answer to your every need.

Calling on Jesus is more effective and powerful than any other thing we can ever say or pray.

The name of Jesus brings protection, provision, peace, healing and salvation.

Demonic spirits are unable to withstand the power the name of Jesus brings into every situation and circumstance.

Every plan that was ever made to upset you, upset your day, is destroyed when we call on the name of Jesus to help us.

My Notes